CELEBRITY HERO

Born In Texas: Hometown Heroes A-Z, Book #3

3

JO GRAFFORD

ISBN: 978-1-944794-94-1

ACKNOWLEDGMENTS

A huge thank you to my editor, Cathleen Weaver, for helping me make this story the best it could be! Plus, another heartfelt thank you goes to my beta readers, Mahasani and Debbie Turner. I also want to give a shout out to my Cuppa Jo Readers on Facebook. Thank you for reading and loving my books!

Join Cuppa Jo Readers at https://www.facebook.com/groups/CuppaJoReaders for sneak peeks, cover reveals, book launches, monthly birthday parties, giveaways, and more!

Free Book!

Also, visit www.JoGrafford.com to sign up for Jo's New Release Newsletter and receive your FREE copy of one of her sweet and clean romance stories!

ABOUT THIS SERIES

Born In Texas: Hometown Heroes A-Z is a sweet and inspirational series of standalone romance stories about small town, everyday heroes. Each title is full of faith and family, hope and love, and always ends in a happily-ever-after!

TITLES:
Accidental Hero
Best Friend Hero

Celebrity Hero

Damaged Hero

Enemies to Hero

Forbidden Hero

Guardian Hero

Hunk and Hero

Instantly Her Hero

Jilted Hero

Kissable Hero

Long Distance Hero

Mistaken Hero

Not Good Enough Hero

Opposites Attract Hero

Playboy Hero

Quiet & Shy Hero

Rockstar Hero

Second Chance Hero

Tortured Hero

Undercover Hero

Volunteer Hero

Workplace Hero

XOXO Hero

Yours Forever Hero

Zillionaire Hero

CHAPTER 1: WHEN THE MUSIC CHANGES

Gabe

Three months earlier

Guilt.

It was something Gabe had lived with for ten straight years — since the day he'd run away from foster care. Not that a foster kid ready to be on his own, in itself, was a bad thing. Leaving his only brother behind in foster care, however, was.

Well, technically, he and Matt were only half brothers, if anyone wanted to split hairs. They shared the same deadbeat dad, as well as the same coffee bean hair and eyes.

The door to his room at the Anderson Ranch B&B abruptly swung open. "Yo! There you are."

Speak of the devil, and he shows up.

Gabe forced what he hoped was a chilled-out older brother smile as he glanced up from the electric piano he'd been fiddling at. Something had been off with his mojo the last few days. Maybe he was still tired after his flight from Nashville, or maybe it was because his agent had just notified him of another three-month-long tour through the Midwest. All he knew was that the words of the song he was supposed to be writing just weren't coming.

"I don't normally barge into a guest room like that, but I've been knocking for a while and, well, the door wasn't locked." As Matt gestured at the rustic pine door with both hands, looking apologetic, the muscles in his darkly tanned arms bulged. He might be the younger brother by two years, but he was by far the strongest. It sort of went with the territory of being a former Army Ranger. In comparison, Gabe imagined his lean and lanky musician's bod looked like a string bean.

"Sorry about that." Gabe didn't know how to explain to his ranch manager brother that musicians didn't hear much besides the words and notes when they were in the middle of composing. "Guess I was completely in the zone." He ran his fingers across the keyboard and pounded out a few stanzas of a short, jazzy number for emphasis. The brothers had only recently been reunited after years of being out of touch, but they were quickly settling into their old brand of camaraderie.

Matt leaned closer to watch him play, looking all relaxed in his blue and white plaid shirt and faded jeans. The cowboy look was a far cry from the Army uniform he'd worn for a good number of years, but it suited him. "That's pretty amazing, actually. I wish I had that kind of talent."

"What? Singing for your dinner like I do?" Gabe teased. It was an understatement, and they both knew it. His last three hit singles had gone platinum, and there were rumors flying around about a forthcoming nomination to the Country Music Hall of Fame.

"No. I was referring to your ability to block everything out." Matt sobered. "Don't get me wrong. I'm not complaining. I have an amazing wife, and a great job. But there are days when the phone won't stop ringing, and folks run in and out of my office all day long like it's a revolving door, and..." He shook his head with a rueful expression. "Shoot! If only I could escape inside my own head like you do. Now *that's* real talent."

Gabe held his younger brother's gaze. "Guess I had plenty of practice while we were growing up. There weren't too many other places to escape to." He tapped a finger against his right temple. "Except here." *That is, until I ran away and left you to fend for yourself in the foster care system.* He'd been longing to bring up the topic for weeks, and the present moment seemed like the perfect opportunity.

"Listen, man." Matt leaned back against the door jamb, looking uncomfortable. "How about we just let the past remain in the past?" He crossed one dusty cowboy boot over the other.

Gabe arched an eyebrow at him. "Does that mean you've forgiven me?"

"For what?" Matt's scowl was genuinely puzzled. He was just that nice of a guy, a far better brother than Gabe deserved.

"For leaving you there alone," Gabe sighed, "without anyone to protect you." It had been eating away at him like acid on the hood of a rusty old truck.

"Oh." Matt snorted out a laugh. "That." He pushed away from the door jamb, smirking. "No offense, dude, but I always thought it was the other way around. You know, me protecting you."

"Hey, now!" Gabe half rose from his black swivel stool, pretending outrage and wishing with all of his might that his brother's claim wasn't true. Which it sadly was. "You're totally forgetting about that time when I stood up to Billy the Bully." He waved a finger, feeling mildly nauseated at the memory. "Remember that? I'd had enough of his garbage and finally told him so." He'd gotten the livin' daylights beaten out of him for his boldness, but Billy had been removed from their foster home that same evening — permanently. Or so Gabe had been told after he'd awakened in a hospital bed with a broken nose and three cracked ribs. As far as he was concerned, though, he'd taken one for the team. Standing up to Billy was something he'd never regret.

"I remember alright." Matt's usual mischievous expression went hard at the memory. "Wish I could forget it, but I can't. I really did think you were going to die that night." He stepped closer to the piano. "I never understood why you got all up in his grill like that. You had to have known you were no match for him — that you didn't stand a chance of winning."

It all depends on your definition of winning. Gabe shuffled the pages of his half-written song, just so he didn't have to continue meeting Matt's gaze. "I guess I figured it was better for him to pick on me than to keep picking on you." He'd never forget that day, either. "I saw him take your lunch earlier in the day."

"It was one stupid PB&J sandwich, Gabe."

"Not true. He'd taken your lunch before," Gabe could feel his brother's eyes on him, "and I couldn't stand the thought of you going hungry. Again." The memory of Matt's way-too-thin eleven-year-old body would be forever etched in his darkest memories.

"Maybe. But it wasn't worth a bunch of broken bones, bro." Matt's voice was so strained with angst that Gabe winced. Still not ready to meet his gaze, Gabe glanced around the room of the B&B where he was staying, soaking in the homey feel of the rustic wood furniture and scattering of rag rugs. Normally he stayed in five-star hotels, so it was a real treat to be sleeping under a homemade quilt each night. If he understood things correctly, the patchwork quilt was one of Bree's creations — Matt's gorgeous blonde and blue-eyed cowgirl wife. *Some guys have all the luck!*

"To me it was worth it," he declared quietly, and he meant it. As the older brother, it had been his unspoken duty to protect Matt, a duty he'd failed at again and again and again. It was the biggest reason he'd finally run away. It wasn't merely to escape the loveless, jail-like environment of their foster home. That he could've handled until he was old enough to leave on legal terms. What he couldn't handle was witnessing the way Matt's youthful optimism was slowly being choked out of him. He couldn't stand to see the hope in his eyes seep away and be replaced by that zombie-blankness that so many foster kids wore like emotional chainmail to hide a childhood of hurt and disillusionment.

So he'd run. And he regretted it to this day.

"Hey." Matt's fist lightly punched Gabe's shoulder. "If forgiveness is what you need, then you can quit worrying, okay? I was never mad at you in the first place, so there's nothing to forgive. To be honest, I was glad when you left."

"Glad!" Gabe finally met his brother's gaze. "Why?" It was the last thing he'd expected Matt to say, and it wasn't making him feel any better.

"Because I didn't think you'd last much longer, that's why," Matt exploded. "Listen, I was born tough. I probably came out of my mother's womb, swinging." His lips twitched. "But you? I'm pretty sure you were already composing your first song on your way into the world."

They shared a strained laugh.

"Nah." Gabe grimaced. "I imagine I was squalling the same as every other poor chap in the nursery."

Matt's smirk returned. "Maybe, but I'm willing to bet you were squalling in key, unlike the rest of us."

Though Gabe smiled, he wasn't ready to let the conversation go. "Okay, so maybe you don't need to hear it, but I need to say it. I'm sorry, Matt. I'm sorry for the way I left. No matter how you try to spin it, it was wrong on every level."

"I turned out alright," Matt protested. "We both did."

No. I didn't. They'd taken drastically different paths in life, and both had beaten the odds of a troubled adolescence that normally led to a troubled adulthood. However, only one of them had found true happiness.

Seeing Gabe's slight head shake, Matt cocked his head sideways. "You know what? Anyone can play Monday morning quarterback about what we coulda, woulda, shoulda done years ago. But you happen to be looking at a guy who met the love of his life while getting pulled over for a speeding ticket. I'm living proof that good things can happen, even in the midst of bad circumstances."

You have no idea how much I envy you. Gabe made a mental note to ask for the whole story sometime about how Matt met Bree, as he stuffed the random sheets of music he'd been scribbling in his black three-ring binder. "Almost makes me want to get out there and put the pedal to the metal, myself." What he wouldn't do to have an incredible woman like Bree to come home to after every band practice and concert! Unlike Matt, however, he didn't possess a mile-wide streak of adventure. Despite the amount of time his career required him to be on the road, he was more of a homebody than a thrill-seeker. A guy who traveled the world but often remained in his hotel room during his spare time to dream, compose music, then put the music to words. It wasn't exactly the recipe for a thriving love life.

"Whatever," Matt scoffed. "I imagine you'll find your Mrs. Right beneath the glow of stage lights."

Gabe turned off his keyboard and shut his three-ring binder, leaving it resting on the music tray in front of him. "I meet lots of women in my line of business, sure." He doubted there was anything he could say to make his younger brother understand what it was really like to walk a day in his shoes. "But there's usually no emotional connection." *As in none whatsoever.* His audience amounted to little more than a sea of faces. Most people couldn't see past the confetti, accolades, and big paycheck of his celebrity lifestyle. They envied his wealth and accomplishments, but they had zero idea what a solitary existence he actually led...what a lonely one.

When Matt settled into troubled silence, Gabe felt a stab of remorse about bringing up such a melancholy topic. "Hey! I know you didn't trot all the way up to the second floor to hear a rich guy bellyaching about how tough he has it." He allowed the irony to seep into his voice.

"I don't think of you as a rich guy." Matt sounded

as troubled as he looked. "You're my brother, and I don't mind listening any time you need a set of ears."

"Thanks." Gabe drew a heavy breath. "Okay. Your turn. Whatcha need from me?"

Matt shrugged, as if what he had to say wasn't all that important. "I just wanted to go over the songs you planned to sing at our upcoming charity concert. Bree and I are putting together a postcard-sized program to hand out to guests at the door."

"Right. About that." Gabe flicked two fingers at his black binder. "I'm experiencing a jag of writer's block. It happens." Again, he didn't expect his brother to understand. "I've been tinkering with a new song all day, and...nothing. It's like I've hit a wall."

Matt nodded, though Gabe knew he was just trying to be nice. "That's cool if you want to come up with some new material for the concert — way cool, actually. But no pressure. Believe me, the locals will be happy no matter what you decide to sing. They're tickled to death just to have you in town. So am I."

"Thanks." Gabe drummed his fingers idly on the silent keys. "There's no way I could say no to such a great cause." Not only did he like the idea of helping raise money for the medical expenses of a few Anderson Ranch employees, it had been a good excuse to pay another visit to his brother. It was only the second time they'd seen each other after years of being apart. Additionally, the B&B at Anderson Ranch had turned out to be the perfect place to rest between singing gigs. However, the fresh country air didn't seem to be having any effect on his current state of writer's block. *Bummer!*

Matt watched his brother intently. "If you take requests, I wouldn't mind hearing you perform *Shootin' the Bull*. I seriously don't have enough time in the day to deal with all the complaints we'll get if you don't at least sing that one."

"Sure thing. No problem." Gabe grinned in appreciation. The song was another one of his own creations.

"Depending on how long you plan to spend on stage, we might even add in some local talent to round out the program."

That was news to Gabe. "I can croon into a microphone for as long as you need me to, bro. All night long, if necessary."

Matt nodded thoughtfully. "We were gunning for ninety minutes with a twenty-minute intermission."

"Done." Gabe's voice was matter-of-fact. He was accustomed to two-hour concerts, so it would be an easy night for him.

"Just let me know if you want me to line up anyone local to sing the opening number for you."

It was the second time Matt had mentioned local talent, so Gabe had to assume his brother already had someone in mind. "I'm accustomed to being a one-man show, but whatever you want, bro. Seriously. I don't mind." *It's your B&B, your event, and your folks we're raising money for.*

Matt winked. "It's no big deal either way. If you prefer to do all the work, we'll be that much more grateful to you at the end of the night."

All the work? Not even. Gabe knew his brother was just being modest. A massive amount of elbow grease went into the logistics of any big event, to include set-up and tear down.

"You can count on me to rock the house with a bunch of fan favorites. And if I can get un-stuck on the song I'm trying to compose, I might be able to debut a brand new title."

Matt's brows rose. "That would be too awesome for words! Are you sure there isn't anything I can do to help?"

"Yeah. Ignore my grumbling. You've already done enough." Gabe waved a hand to take in their surroundings. "You put me in a room with a view." And on short notice, too. He'd arrived about twenty hours ago in the middle of the night. Every time he glanced out the window, he soaked up the beauty of the mesas and canyons. "A little R&R should nudge me right out of my slump." And then the words would finally start flowing again.

Words, words, words. I need words! The musical notes had been the easy part. He literally breathed music from the time he awoke each morning until he laid his head on the pillow again each night. What he was missing was...

I don't know. Over the past few months, a bleak-ness had set in that he couldn't seem to shake. He needed a change of pace, change of scenery, or change of something he hadn't yet put his finger on to get his creative mojo flowing again.

A sly look had stolen across Matt's face as he patiently listened to Gabe's frustrated tirade. "If it's inspiration you're looking for, Music Man, I may have an idea, after all."

Gabe's interest piqued. "I'm all ears."

"We have a maid on staff who has a pretty incredible voice. She sings while she works, and it's worth listening to. No joke. Our guests claim it's like getting a mini-concert every time she cleans a room."

"Nice." Gabe's interest had waned at the mention of the woman's vocation. Lots of people sang in the shower or whistled while they worked. Though his brother meant well, Gabe wasn't too interested in having his ears jangled by some pitch-y rendition of the latest pop song.

"Thanks, man. I'll be sure to tune in the next time your multi-talented maid yodels her way down the hall."

"You won't be disappointed." Matt swiveled toward the door. "Oh, one more thing." He half-turned around. "Bree told me to invite you to our staff dinner this evening. It's a lot less formal than it sounds. Everybody is like family around here."

"Yeah, I noticed. Tell Bree I said thanks." Gabe was careful to stop short of making any promises. His mind was already racing ahead to what he planned on doing next in the effort to jolt his musical talent back in gear. Maybe he'd go on a trail ride. He couldn't exactly take his keyboard on the back of a horse, but he had perfect pitch. He could hum or sing his way through the music after he plucked the right words from the air. *Yep. That's it.* He could already feel the power of the horse beneath him and the dry wind riffling his hair and clothing as he clip-clopped toward the canyon rim.

"Alright, then. I'll scoot for now. Looks like you might already be back in the zone." Matt's brown eyes were twinkling as he turned away. "See you tonight. Six-thirty-ish." He waved two tanned fingers in the air instead of saying goodbye.

Gabe glanced down at his watch as he moved toward the window. It was only three o'clock in the afternoon, plenty of time to squeeze in a trail ride before dinner. He leaned against the side of the window frame, peering out at the majestic canyons stretching on for miles — endless sandy rises and drop-offs with streaks of brown and red clay. Tumble-weeds rolled aimlessly this way and that in the breeze, and the occasional burst of greenery from a pine or spruce offered the only varying pop of color.

After a moment's reflection, he realized seeing wasn't enough. A musician like him was never content to simply look; he needed to hear the music of the wind and the sounds of farm life to fully appreciate the scene unfolding before him.

Reaching for the latch, he unlocked the window and lifted it. The breeze outside immediately swirled past him into the guest room, scattering the short stack of full-color brochures that had been so artfully displayed on the T.V. credenza. His menu options and available ranch activities drifted to the hardwood floor in a series of papery thuds.

Making a mental note to pick them up later, Gabe leaned his hands on the windowsill and allowed the peace of the country to sink into his bones. There were cows mooing in the distance, the cluck of hens, and the low rumble of motors as two ranch hands rode past on tractors. A minute or two passed before his ears picked up a new sound — that of a female singing.

The alto voice started at a low hum, one that was surprisingly in key. Then she launched into the words of a familiar country western song about the miracle of love. It wasn't necessarily a romantic song; it could've been a song a mother sang to her child or a friend to a friend. It was about pure love, the kind between people who mattered to each other, the kind that made the other person's life richer for it. Gabe had always dreamed about being close to someone like that some day, though he'd not yet experienced it.

This woman, however, had. He instinctively knew that she was singing the song about someone she cared for. There was no other way the words could've held so much feeling. They were sweetly poignant, yet powerful. Muted with sadness, yet tinged with hope. Her voice soared to a higher set of notes that required a little more volume to hit them exactly right.

Unable to resist the temptation, Gabe closed his eyes and pretended the woman was singing directly to him. He allowed her voice to surround him, tug at his senses, and sweep him away by its beauty. *Man!* A voice like that was pure magic. It stirred his emotions and instantly made him feel more alive. An inexplicable wave of energy coursed through him, pulsing with the need to break free.

Without warning, the dam inside him broke. The wall that had been holding back his creativity for days crumbled.

You were right, Matt. Your singing maid was the exact elixir I needed to restore my musical soul. Gabe had no doubt he'd stumbled across the voice of the very woman that the B&B guests were always bragging about.

Opening his eyes, he left the window and strode back to his keyboard. Hitting the power button, he watched as the settings on the control panel lit up like dozens of tiny red Christmas tree lights. He hastily punched a few buttons to add the faint drone of string instruments in the background behind the grand piano setting he'd been composing on earlier.

Then he started to mouth the words that had been missing from his song. It was called *Under the Texas Stars*. Every few seconds he paused to write down the words that were flowing from his mind to his hand. The page in his black notebook quickly filled. In less than ten minutes, the entire song was complete.

Afterward, he closed his notebook and turned off his keyboard. He always took a break after composing a new song. It gave the freshly inspired words and notes time to really resonate inside him. He would return later to tweak, edit, and polish the song before testing it out on a live audience.

Though he moved back to the window, Gabe could no longer hear the woman singing. He was disappointed, but he had a plan. The rest of his band, The Texans, weren't scheduled to arrive for another twenty-four hours, so he had plenty of time to track down the woman behind the voice that had inspired him to write it.

Dinner. She'll be at Matt and Bree's staff dinner. Gabe was sure of it. *Guess I'll be accepting that invitation, after all.*

He went on the trail ride he'd planned earlier, mainly to pass the time. Then he showered and changed. There was no point in trying to fade in with the ranch hands. Jeans and boots were a given. Instead of a t-shirt or a plaid shirt, however, he selected a black, long-sleeved button-up shirt and clapped on a white felt Stetson to go with it. When Matt's singing maid first laid eyes on him, she needed to see him as the successful country singer that he was.

She might be currently working as a maid, but she was a star in the making. He planned to talk her into letting him showcase her talent during the opening number of the upcoming charity concert.

Wondering what her name was and what she looked like, he left his room and headed for the stairs. Jogging down them, he traversed the wide waiting area in front of the busy dining room. Not only did the B&B guests patronize the restaurant, folks from all over town flocked there each evening to sink their teeth into the Anderson's famous t-bone steaks.

This evening, the white linen draped tables were ablaze with flameless candles set in iron wagon wheel centerpieces. The scent of smoked meat, simmering chili, and fresh-baked bread swirled through the air, mingling with the chatter of happy patrons.

Gabe reached the silver *Authorized Personnel Only* door leading inside the kitchen. Pushing it open, he stepped inside and nearly collided with a tall, slender blonde who was heading in the opposite direction — out.

"Whoa! Sorry about that. Are you okay?" He reached for her shoulders, surprised at how strong and sturdy they felt beneath the thin fabric of her red, white, and blue plaid shirt. She wasn't nearly as delicate as she looked, despite her haunted expression and the faint purplish-blue shadows beneath her eyes.

Most women of his acquaintance would have covered the shadows with make-up. Not this woman. It didn't look like she was wearing any makeup at all.

Though her face remained averted, he couldn't help admiring the curve of her cheekbone and her perfectly peachy skin. The cornrow braids falling from beneath her Stetson were an interesting touch, though. He'd only seen major athletes sporting the look before now.

"I'm fine." The lack of warmth in her tone made Gabe abruptly drop his hands.

"It's you." He had no trouble recognizing her rich, melodic voice as the one he'd overheard through his open window. His heartbeat pounded at the realization that he was facing the very woman he'd been hoping to meet this evening, and she was even more lovely than he'd anticipated.

Her expression seemed to freeze. "Um, have we met before?" She tipped her face up to his to fully meet his gaze, and he was forced to revise his earlier opinion of her. No, her skin wasn't as peachy perfect as he'd originally presumed. A pink, puckered scar began in the middle of her cheek and extended to the underside of her chin. It was too wide and asymmetrical to be from a cut. He was guessing it had been caused by some sort of burn — one that added to, rather than took away from, her haunting beauty.

"Not exactly." He took a step back, sensing she'd appreciate a little more breathing room after their near collision. "I overheard you singing earlier."

Her lush lips twisted. "I reckon putting a face to the voice is a real let-down for you, huh?"

"What?" He was floored by the bitterness lacing

her words. "You've gotta be kidding! I was blown away by your talent, Miss...ah..."

"Shiloh Neeson," she supplied curtly. "An ex-Marine turned maid, who doesn't require her corn to be buttered by a bunch of meaningless compliments." Her voice was flat and unemotional. "I only sing to keep the customers happy. You know...job security."

Without giving him a chance to respond, she moved around him with her braids rustling like serpents around her shoulders.

He spun around to stare after her, but the only thing he saw was the silver door swinging into place.

"Told you," his brother sang out in an amused voice from behind him.

Gabe slowly turned around. "Help me out here. I don't even know what I did wrong."

"Nothing." Matt stepped forward to jovially sling an arm across his shoulders. "She just takes a little time and patience. Like I said before, though, she's worth the wait."

CHAPTER 2: SNAP, CRACKLE, AND ROCK!

Shiloh

Shiloh knew she was being rude to Gabe Romero as she stomped her way out of Bree's kitchen with its enticing scent of made-from-scratch Italian pizza. It was at least partly his fault, though. The way the celebrity country western singer had been looking at her scarred cheek had rubbed her entirely the wrong way. She was a tough gal who could take care of herself in just about any situation, preferably with a weapon in hand. There was one thing she didn't deal well with, though, and that was a pity.

Not that she wasn't a pitiful sight. With a breathy sigh, she glanced down at her faded jeans and scuffed boots, the standard uniform for just about every job at the Anderson Ranch B&B. Guests came there for the canyon views and wilderness experience, so even the maids got to wear Stetsons. *Lucky me!* She was fortunate she wasn't required to dress up, because her minuscule wardrobe was running on the threadbare side these days. Every item of clothing she owned had come from yard sales and second-hand shops. *Gosh!* It was the story of her life — working like the dickens but never quite getting ahead.

Trying to break the vicious cycle of poverty the Neeson family had always been stuck on, was the main reason she'd enlisted in the Marines. Sure, it would've been more fun to attend college and study music like Gabe Romero's online bio said he had, but poor chicks like her didn't have those kinds of options. She was the daughter of a seasonal farm hand, who also happened to be a single dad, so she'd needed to start producing a paycheck right after high school — not only to keep food on the table, but also to help finish putting her younger sister, Shayley, through school.

Sadly, her commander hadn't hesitated to medically board her out of the Marines after that fateful ambush in Kandahar. Her PTSD had been so extreme that they'd stamped her records *unfit for duty*, then sent her home for ongoing treatment through the VA Health Care System.

Unfortunately, they'd sent her back to a father who'd passed away shortly after her return, back to the poverty she'd fought so hard to escape, and back to a pregnant younger sister.

Reaching the door of the second-floor room the two of them shared at the B&B, Shiloh gave a light warning knock to announce her arrival. Then she opened the door and stepped inside. The sight that met her made her lips tighten.

"What are you doing?" she cried, shutting the door firmly behind her.

"I'm finished with my nap," Shayley announced cheerfully. She was lying on her side atop a rectangular rag rug, doing leg lifts. "Just working out the kinks." She was as cute as a button in her pink maternity tunic and black leggings. Her long, blonde hair was pulled back in a pair of French braids that were hanging to the floor, and her swollen belly made Shiloh think of a large dollop of berry ice cream spilling from an overturned cone.

"No one said anything about napping." Shiloh slapped her hands on her hips, studying her sister critically. "I specifically remember your doctor using the word *rest*. How is this resting?" Just thinking about how sick Shayley had been not too long ago, made her mouth go dry with worry. Keeping an eye on her baby sister was the whole reason she'd given up her job as a security guard to come work at Anderson Ranch. Well, that, and to take over most of her sister's maid duties until she could deliver the baby and get back on her feet. That was going to be awhile yet, considering she was only in her second trimester.

"Okay. You caught me." Shayley sat up with a sigh. "I'm not resting." She leisurely stretched her arms high over her head and pivoted her body from side to side. "Wow! That feels good." Then she lowered her arms. "I know you mean well, Shy, but I'm sick and tired of resting." Her lower lip came out in a pout. "No offense, but ever since you moved to the ranch, I've spent so much time in this blasted room that it's starting to feel like a jail."

"No offense taken," Shiloh snapped. *Are you kidding me?* What right did her sister have to complain? *Everything I do is for you, chickadee.*

"Speaking of which..." Shayley paused her toe touches to shoot a sly look up at her older sister from beneath her ridiculously long lashes. "Even in jail, prisoners get let out of their cells now and then for a break. Foster said so."

"Foster!" Shiloh muttered, stepping farther into the room. "Taking advice from a jailbird over a doctor. Nice going, Shayley." Tossing her Stetson on her bed, she flopped down beside it and leaned back against the headboard, careful to keep the soles of her boots hanging over the edge. Though it was dinnertime, she was far from off-duty. Her job at the B&B was no 9:00 to 5:00 gig. It was one of those round-the-clock, always-on-call sorta things. To be fair, though, everyone on the ranch pitched in after hours if a guest needed something, including the owners — Brody Anderson and Bree and Matt Romero.

"That's not fair, and you know it!" Shayley protested. She rocked back and forth a few times for momentum, then curled her lithe figure forward to her feet. "Foster isn't that bad. He may have made some poor decisions in the past. I mean, who hasn't? But he's a good person. Always has been and always will be."

"So you keep reminding me." Shiloh grimaced, knowing her sister was referring to the reason Foster Kane had spent a few years in jail. Though he swore up and down he'd never done drugs, he'd spent his teen years hanging with the wrong crowd, and he'd been in the car the night they got busted for possession. Most unfortunately, all of this had happened while Shiloh was serving overseas in harm's way alongside his older brother, a fellow Marine named Samson. So, call her hard-nosed and unforgiving, but she didn't have a whole lot of sympathy to spare for Samson's younger rebel brother.

"He's family now." Shayley's voice grew defensive. She padded barefoot across the room to the vanity resting outside their bathroom. Bending over the sink, she turned on the faucet and splashed water on her face. "He's in our lives to stay; you may as well accept it."

"You mean he's in your life," Shiloh corrected. "Can't say that I'm overly thrilled about the way he's always hovering like a helicopter around you." Sorry, but she plumb wasn't ready to call him family. Sure, Foster's older brother was the father of Shayley's baby, but he'd never bothered putting a ring on her finger. He'd sadly deteriorated into one of those anti-government, off-the-grid kind of guys, who claimed a stupid piece of paper wouldn't make them any more married.

He was as wrong as a horse's tail on a pig, of course, and Shiloh had every intention of having a come-to-Jesus talk with him soon on the matter. She honestly didn't care how off-the-grid he chose to live; but now that he was about to become a father, he was going to stand before a justice of the peace and do the right thing by her sister, if Shiloh had to drag his oversized carcass all the way to Town Hall herself.

Shayley dried her face on a hand towel and padded across the narrow foyer to yank open their closet door. "Foster doesn't hover. He's just looking out for me while I'm away from home, like Samson made him promise to." Her voice shook at the mention of the man she loved. It was clear that she missed him.

Shiloh muffled a snort. As much as she respected the guy as a fellow soldier, she truly had no idea what her younger sister saw in him romantically. He was short-tempered and mouthy, not to mention a nauseating conspiracy theorist. It was as if the war had addled his brains. He'd not been the same since his return from overseas.

She blew out a frustrated breath that made the bangs rise on her forehead. "I never liked how Samson simply assigned you to Foster's care." *The gall of him!* "Sometimes I think he forgets we're not still in the military." It was one thing to follow orders as a Marine during battle, but it was another thing

entirely for Samson to come home and recruit his
own para-military group on the property next door to
Anderson Ranch. Sure, he was also running a
bonafide business of hard-nosed security guards (all
former soldiers), but there were times when Shiloh
worried that he was crossing a line with all his anti-
government rhetoric. And he'd certainly crossed a
line when he'd fallen in love with her baby sister and
gotten her pregnant before legally joining their hands
in marriage.

All of her gripes aside about Samson Kane,
though, Shiloh would never forget that she owed the
man her life. He was the reason she'd escaped the
explosion in Kandahar, with no more than a scar on
her face and a hefty case of PTSD. He'd literally run
through fire to save her, incurring serious wounds
that had been steadily taking their toll on his health
ever since. She was worried about him, plain and
simple — worried about him in ways that she didn't
dare confide in her sister. Shayley had enough on her
plate, dealing with their unplanned pregnancy.

She rummaged through the small closet they
shared and came out waving a pale blue sundress on a
hangar. "That's just how Samson is. Once a Marine,
always a Marine, I guess. You're a lot like that, too,
you know. Always ordering me around and stuff." She
gave a wry chuckle. "Then again, that started long
before you joined the Marines."

"Ha ha," Shiloh muttered dryly. She tipped her
head back against the headboard, closing her eyes.

When a flutter of fabric landed on her arms and chest, however, she jolted upright.

"Sheesh, Shayley! You should know better than to pull a stunt like that." Soldiers with PTSD had been known to come up swinging for less provocation.

Shayley was standing over her, holding the blue sundress against her faded shirt and jeans. "Whatever. You would never hurt me, Shy."

She sounded so confident and unconcerned that Shiloh felt her eyes grow damp. *And that's why I love you so much, chickadee.* To cover her emotion, she demanded, "What are you doing?"

"Helping you dress for dinner."

"I'm already dressed." Shiloh tried to push the sundress away, but Shayley stubbornly held it in place. *Oh, my lands, kid! Just leave me alone.* She'd already grabbed a slice of pizza and eaten it on the go, and she'd been planning on delivering a dinner tray to Shayley when she awoke from her nap.

"I really do think blue is your color."

"Here and I thought it was plaid." Shiloh rolled her eyes.

"Funny."

"Believe me, I've been called worse."

"I know. By me. Many times." Shayley grinned. "Behind your back, in my head, in your face, whatever time and place suited me."

"I am aware." Shiloh shook her head. Their relationship for too many years had been more like a substitute mom and daughter, rather than two sisters. "What's your point?"

"My point is that I'm ready to blow this popsicle stand. And since I know neither you nor Foster is going to let me out of your sight without a big brouhaha, you're going to be escorting me to dinner, General Neeson."

"I've already eaten."

"I haven't. And before you offer to go grab some food for me, the answer is no. I'm leaving this room, Shy, like it or not. I'm pregnant, not crippled. I'm going to eat dinner, and then I'm going to have Foster drive me next door for a long overdue visit with my hubby."

Her tone was so final that Shiloh realized there was no point in continuing their argument. The Neeson girls were two peas in a pod when it came to stubbornness.

"If you insist, little mama." Shiloh swung her legs to the floor and stood.

"I do, so put on the dress," her sister ordered, holding it out again. "You've had that same shirt on for days."

Shiloh gaped at her. "I have not! That's disgusting." Sure, she cycled her way through her tiny wardrobe pretty quickly, but sheesh! She always washed her clothes before rewearing them.

"Well, you may as well be. All that plaid is making me nauseous. Please, please, *please* wear something else to dinner tonight."

"Oh, for Pete's sake! Give it to me." Shiloh snatched the sundress from her sister and headed toward the bathroom. "But I'm not taking off my boots no matter how much you complain."

"Fine!" Shayley shouted at her retreating shoulders.

"Fine!" Shiloh hollered back. Though she refused to give her sister the satisfaction of hearing her laugh out loud, her lips were twitching. It actually felt good to know Shayley was feeling well enough to engage in sisterly spats again. She'd seriously been so beat down lately, between her bout of sickness and Samson's refusal to visit her at the ranch (claiming it was too on-the-grid), that Shiloh had been worrying non-stop about her and the baby.

Slamming the bathroom door a little harder than necessary, she proceeded to strip off her workaday shirt and jeans, which *did* require the temporary removal of her boots. She actually didn't have anything against shedding her boots for dinner. The problem was she hadn't taken the time to acquire any other footwear, because she'd not expected to be at the B&B this long. Her original plan was to merely cover Shayley's maid duties until she recovered from her illness, then return to her security job with the Kanes next door. But that hadn't happened.

Shayley's doctor was making noises about putting her on permanent bed rest because of her elevated blood pressure, and she needed to keep her job to maintain her medical insurance. *So here I remain.* Shiloh slid the borrowed sundress over her head and let the length of it settle to her knees. The woman staring back at her in the mirror seemed suddenly younger — sixteen again instead of her twenty-six years. Her cornrow braids also suddenly looked too severe for the occasion.

I can't believe I'm doing this. Reaching behind her, Shiloh pulled the snarl of braids over her shoulder. Then she slid the stretch bands from the end of each one, swiftly unbraiding her hair. The result was a rippling set of blonde waves. She riffled her fingers through them to loosen them a bit, fluffing them out and giving them more volume. Stepping back into her boots, she surveyed her reflection in the mirror one last time, hardly recognizing the much softer, more feminine version of herself.

Bracing for the inevitable outburst from her sister, she gingerly turned the doorknob and stepped back into their bedroom.

She found Shayley perched on her bed on the other side of the room. "Nice!" She clapped her hands in girlish delight.

"Happy now?" Shiloh inquired, giving her a sarcastic bow.

"Yes, yes, and more yes!" She clasped her hands under her chin and stared in amazement. "That's what I'm talking about, girl. You look so...wait a sec." She sprang to her feet, with an agility that belied her condition, and yanked open the top drawer of the nightstand between their beds.

When Shiloh saw the makeup kit in her hands, she shook her head. "Nope. Negatory. You already got your way. I'm wearing a dress, but I strictly draw the line on being painted up like a clown."

"You sorely underestimate my skills as a makeup artist." Shayley advanced on her, brandishing the brush that she'd already dipped in face powder. "Not to mention, you're supposed to be helping me keep my stress level down, not constantly picking fights with me."

Shiloh's jaw dropped. The shoe was so on the other foot. "Me? Constantly picking—" She bit back her words as Shayley reached her and started dusting her nose with the creamy powder.

"Omigosh! Stop." Coughing, Shiloh waved away the small cloud of powder. "I think I'm allergic to that stuff."

"Nice try," Shayley kept applying the powder, "but no woman is allergic to being beautiful." She took extra care as she painted and dusted makeup over the scar on Shiloh's cheek.

Hoping it wasn't because her baby sister was secretly ashamed of her damaged face, Shiloh glumly held still while Shayley added mascara, blush, and a dash of lip gloss. "You're killing me, Shay. Truly killing me."

"Yeah, I'm awesome like that," Shayley retorted cheerfully. Applying a second coat of lip gloss, she stepped back and cocked her head to one side, critically studying her work. "There. Now you're almost as awesome as me."

"Thanks, I think." Shiloh shook her head despairingly at her sister.

"And now you can quit being so jealous of Foster, since he'll probably only have eyes for you tonight."

"You think I'm jealous?" Shiloh snorted. "Not even. He's way too young for me." She was pretty sure he was closer to Shayley's twenty-one years than her own twenty-six. "And I've long suspected all other women cease to exist when you're in the room, sis."

Shayley smoothed her hands over the pink fabric covering her blooming belly. "You really shouldn't say stuff like that. He's my brother-in-law, Shy. How about we just leave it at that?"

"If he will, I will," she retorted with a scowl.

"What's that supposed to mean?"

"That I suspect he cares for you a little more than a brother-in-law should." Or a lot more.

For the next several seconds, they were locked in a glaring contest. It was something they'd done many times in the past, daring the other to be the first to break down and snicker.

A knock sounded at their door. "Shay? You in there?" It was Foster's voice.

"Well, what do you know?" Shiloh muttered.

Shayley laughed first, but Shiloh joined in.

"I heard that," he declared, making them laugh harder.

Shayley sailed across the room to open the door,

and there he stood, all cowboy rugged and too good looking for his own good. His ripped arms and chest were stuffed into a plain white t-shirt that was only half-tucked into a pair of faded jeans. He was wearing one of those ridiculously large belt buckles that generally meant a guy had done something supremely stupid at a rodeo — like ridden a bull longer than anyone else at the event and lived to talk about it.

"Hey." It was one simple, innocuous-sounding word, but his low, husky voice made it seem more intimate. He was so busy drinking in Shayley's pregnant girl cuteness, that he hadn't yet noticed Shiloh was in a dress. That was telling.

"Where have you been?" Shayley stepped closer to him and stretched to her tiptoes to kiss his cheek.

There was something so raw and fiercely defensive in his expression as he locked gazes with Shiloh over her shoulder, that she had to revise her opinion of him. Foster Kane most definitely harbored more than brotherly feelings for her sister. Every instinct in her was screaming that he was hopelessly in love with his brother's wife-in-name-only. What a big, freaking mess!

To his credit, his arms never left his sides as Shayley went through her usual routine of chattering and fluttering around him. "I figured I could count on you, of all people, to spring me out of jail. But, noooo! You were MIA all afternoon, mister."

He shrugged, though the look in his piercing brown eyes softened at her teasing. "Shiloh said you needed your rest." His jaw tightened. "And I'm pretty sure Samson would agree." The ironclad finality in his voice was all Shiloh needed to hear. She knew with sudden certainty that, no matter what feelings he harbored for his sister-in-law, he had no intention of acting on them and betraying his brother. Maybe Shiloh had been a little too quick to write off Foster; there might be more to him, after all.

Reluctant admiration infused her as she met his gaze and gave him a single, hard nod. *Thanks*, she mouthed, appreciating how he hadn't hesitated to back her up when it came to Shayley's health.

Shayley's lower lip trembled at his words, though, making Shiloh want to march next door and shake Samson until his ears rattled. How dare he continue his stupid off-the-grid shenanigans while he had a baby on the way! Her sister missed his stubborn hide like crazy. He should be visiting her every single day!

Blinking rapidly, Shayley murmured, "Will you at least take me to see him after dinner?"

"You know I will." Foster angled his head at the hallway behind him. "You ready to hit the chow line now?"

"Way ready." She sashayed ahead of him and headed for the stairs.

He jogged to catch up, stepped around her, and playfully spread his arms to herd her back toward the elevator.

"You, too?" She pouted.

"Just doing my job." His smile was mocking as he stepped closer, still flapping his arms like an eagle.

"I'm not your job, cowboy. I'm your family." But she didn't fight him as he ushered the three of them down the gleaming hardwood hallway.

Once inside the elevator, he gave Shiloh a sideways glance. "Nice dress."

Oh, so you did notice it, eh? "Shayley made me wear it." She rolled her shoulders, feeling suddenly conspicuous and wishing like crazy that she was back in her jeans.

"You're welcome," Shayley sang out cheerfully, not hesitating to take credit for the remarkable transformation in her sister.

Shiloh rolled her eyes but didn't respond. She'd started wearing her hair in tight cornrows during her stint in the Marines, liking how they kept her hair firmly out of her face. Plus, they were easier to keep clean during extended periods of time in the field. They were also delightfully off-putting. The style had a don't-mess-with-me feel to it that suited her so much more than the fluffy, come-hither waves she was wearing this evening.

For some inexplicable reason, her thoughts jumped back to the dreamy Gabe Romero with his soulful dark eyes.

Don't go there, she inwardly commanded herself. *Don't.* Her life was complicated enough; the last thing she needed was to go gaga over some crazy gorgeous celebrity who was way out of her league.

The elevator doors rolled open to the front of the B&B, which doubled as a check-in area for guests and a waiting area for the B&B's popular steak restaurant.

Foster swung out one long arm to hold open the elevator for both sisters. As Shiloh passed by him, he muttered, "You really do look nice."

She shrugged. "It's just a dress."

He shook his head, admiration glinting in his dark gaze. "Nope. It's a Neeson girl in a dress." He waggled his brows at her. "Something I don't get to see very often, and it's really hot."

Shiloh wondered if he even realized that his gaze had snapped back to her sister.

"Was I right, or was I right, Shy?" Shayley bragged as they traversed the waiting area with its comfy leather furniture and cowhide rugs. "I have another prediction to make. Every single guy in the building is going to be begging for your number tonight."

"Good gracious! I sure hope not." Shaking her head, Shiloh trudged ahead of them, across the front of the restaurant. Its white linen dressed tables, glimmering with candlelight, were crammed to overflowing with patrons. Avoiding eye contact in case any of them recognized her and tried to flag her down, she made a quick detour through the silver door on the right that led to Bree's kitchen.

The moment she stepped inside, Gabe's rich tenor voice assailed her. It was pure country gold with a raw, rocky edge. The song he was singing, though, was one she didn't recognize.

He and his brother were perched on horse saddle stools at the bar in the back of the kitchen, where the ranch hands often took their meals. Each of the stools was custom-built from a repurposed Anderson Ranch saddle, one of Bree's latest crafty creations.

Crew Anderson, who was Brody and Bree's cousin, and two other ranch hands, Nash and Zane Wilder, were on their feet, clapping out the beat and two-stepping to the song.

Gabe was straddling his stool, with his shiny black boots hooked casually through the silver stirrup rungs below. As his voice de-crescendoed through the last line of the song, "So many stars that I lose myself in them," he glanced up. He went still at the sight of Shiloh, though he repeated the last line and ended on a high note before going silent.

His brother and friends broke into whistles and clapping. Foster and Shayley joined in as they stepped closer.

Matt Romero clapped the longest and loudest for his brother. "Nothing like having your own mini-concert over dinner from the best country western singer on the planet." There was no denying the pride in his voice.

Shiloh alone held back from approaching the bar, riveted as much by her own tangle of emotions as she was by the beauty of the song. She'd secretly been a fan of Gabe and The Texans for years, and his in-person voice and presence definitely lived up to her fan-girl fantasies. He was the real deal. There was no lip syncing and heavy-handed editing, like so many other musicians did to cover their pitchiness or limited voice ranges. No doubt about it, Gabe Romero could sing!

Following his brother's slightly dazed line of sight, Matt glanced over his shoulder at her. "Hey, Shiloh! Whatcha think of Gabe's new song?"

Her eyes widened in astonishment. "You wrote that?" She finally allowed herself to fully meet Gabe's curious, searching gaze. Man, but he looked every shade of hunky in that all-black button-up shirt of his.

He gave her a smile that felt surprisingly shy. "Yeah, I scribble out most of my own tunes."

"Wow!" She felt her cheeks heat with embarrassment. It was something she probably would've known if she'd bothered to browse his website or social media accounts.

He didn't seem to notice her discomfort. "So, do you like it?" he prodded.

She nodded and gave him an emphatic, "No."

The expressions of nearly everyone in the room froze.

"Oh, come on, y'all." She rolled her eyes. "I don't just like it. I absolutely love it!" *Loosen up. Sheesh! Gabe might be a celebrity, but he's a real person.* Her gut told her he'd probably appreciate being treated like one, too.

The answering glint in his eyes told her she was right.

"High praise, indeed, coming from our resident

maestro." Matt reached over and high-fived his brother. "In case you haven't guessed, she's the local talent I was telling you about. So, if you're looking for someone to sing the opening song with you at our concert..." His dark eyes twinkled as he let his suggestion sink in.

It was Shiloh's turn to freeze. Her gaze flickered in alarm to Matt's. He might be her boss, but what he was suggesting was way outside of her job description. "I'm more of a sing-in-the-shower kinda gal. I don't think I was made for the spotlight."

"Bull!" His chin jutted in defiance. "You sing for our guests all the time."

"That's different," she protested.

"How?"

"It's just one or two people at a time. Nothing like the size of audiences Gabe and his Texans are accustomed to performing for."

Gabe shrugged, finally chiming into the conversation. "I could coach you on a few techniques for how to curb stage fright."

Stage fright? She stared at him, aghast at the realization that he assumed she was afraid of a few gazillion staring eyes. "Thanks. I'm hugely flattered, but I can't," she informed him flatly, hoping that would be the end of it.

"Oh, come on!" Shayley piped up from the other end of the bar. She and Foster were perched side-by-side on the saddle stools, each holding a slice of Bree's scrumptious, made-from-scratch pizza. "It's for a good cause, you know." Her voice grew thready with emotion over the knowledge that the proceeds of the concert would help pay the medical bills both she and Foster Kane had incurred before their new medical insurance benefits kicked in.

Shiloh gave her sister a beseeching look. Surely she remembered Shiloh's reasons for wanting to stay out of the limelight; she didn't need her physical whereabouts discovered by one man in particular.

As if reading her thoughts, Shayley slid down from her stool to come hug Shiloh. "I know you're worried about that creep finding you," she murmured in her ear, "but it's been over two years. He's probably long gone by now."

Shayley was one of the few people Shiloh had confided in about her stalker, and the fact that he was a fellow soldier who'd served overseas with her and Samson. The same guy who, in hindsight, may have actually started the fire that had claimed the lives of two other soldiers and left Samson fighting for his.

"While you trade sisterly secrets over there, let me just say this." Matt's voice drifted over them with quiet somberness. "As you're well aware, Shiloh, this charity concert is about helping out some of our own. Though I won't try to force your hand if you really don't want to sing on stage, everyone else is pitching in, and I can't think of a finer way for you to contribute than by sharing your incredible voice."

As Shiloh continued to hesitate, Shayley squeezed her shoulders. "Please, Shy. Do it for me."

That's so not fair of you! Knowing it was something she would probably regret later, Shiloh reluctantly nodded. "Well, how can I say no to that?"

"You can't." Gabe beckoned her forward, dark eyes shining. "How about we give 'em a taste of what's coming, eh?" His gaze swept appreciatively over her sundress, bare knees, and cowgirl boots before returning to her face.

She had to force her feet to move forward. "Sure. I guess. But I have a few conditions." She strove for a casual tone but wasn't sure if she succeeded.

"Cool! Whatcha need, maestro?" Gabe's voice was teasing, making her insides go all soft and fluttery.

"Just keep me out of the spotlight, okay? And keep my name out of it, too. As in don't speak it, and don't print it, alright?"

Gabe's gaze narrowed on hers. "Got a bounty on your head, huh?"

"Something like that." She raised her chin, not giving any ground. "Do we have a deal?"

"Yep." His expression relaxed, and he changed the subject — thankfully. "I know you know this song, since I heard you singing it earlier." He winked at her, a fun and flirtatious gesture that made her knees go weak. Then he sang the opening lines.

She waited until the end of the verse to join in. Then she stepped closer to him and launched full throttle into the chorus. Their voices rose in a perfect blend of harmonies. It was as if they'd been born to sing together.

For the space of a few breathtaking minutes, Shiloh allowed herself to be swept away by it all — to forget the darkness of her past and to bask in the present. She sang directly into the dark, brooding eyes of Gabe freaking Romero of The Texans, living out one of her biggest, longest-held daydreams.

The achingly beautiful music made her scars dim — both inside and out — and she was happy to be alive, to be with him, to simply...be.

CHAPTER 3: CAT AND MOUSE

Gabe

Gabe couldn't remember ever feeling this exhilarated anywhere off stage. Normally it took strobe lights, rolling cameras, and a cheering crowd to get him this pumped. He lived for the thrill of performing. It was the only thing that had proven powerful enough to fill the empty parts of him.

Until today.

Until Shiloh Neeson had captured his attention through his open window earlier with her siren song.

Until now, while she was standing in front of him with her voice soaring alongside his.

He didn't want the song to end and didn't want to break eye contact when it did. Gazing into each other's eyes while singing, had created a connection that was truly electrifying, at least on his part. He'd never sung a finer set of notes than he did during the magic of those few minutes.

After the final words of the song faded into

silence, their audience of family and friends broke into whoops, whistles, and clapping. Gabe still couldn't bring himself to look away from Shiloh. Her lips were parted, and her blue-gray eyes were shining into his. A faint tinge of pink rode her cheeks that hadn't been there before. It wasn't exactly a blush, but it was more than the indifference she'd shown to him during their first encounter. It was...something.

Well aware of their interested audience, he gave her a short nod. "Not bad. Not bad at all." Man, but her long blonde waves tonight made her look like an entirely different woman than the one who'd been wearing such tight cornrows only a few hours earlier. She was every shade of smoking hot in that sundress, too. On some women, it might have simply looked soft and feminine. On her, however, it drew the viewer's gaze to the sculpted planes of her neck and shoulders. She radiated strength and resilience from the inside out. Gabe couldn't help wondering what it would feel like to have a former soldier like her in his arms.

"Not bad?" Matt exploded, treating him to an are-you-crazy look. "You two sounded incredible together. You're gonna rock the house during our concert. Isn't that right, baby?"

His wife, who had moved across the room to pull a pair of silver trays out of her commercial-grade ovens, returned bearing one of the trays. "Yes! A bazillion times yes, which I happen to think is cause for a celebration. Or dessert, at least." Bree beamed a satisfied smile in Shiloh's direction. "The first serving goes to our newest starlet."

Gabe watched as Shiloh's expression became shuttered at the compliment. She silently accepted the white mug of lava cake Bree set in front of her on the bar and forced a smile as Bree poured an extra drizzle of chocolate sauce over it. However, she barely touched it. By not meeting anyone's gaze or participating in any of the conversations zinging back and forth between the rest of the jovial staff members, she seemed to be trying to fade out of the limelight as quickly as she'd blossomed into it.

Not quite ready to let go of the exuberance they'd experienced together while singing, Gabe leaned across the bar to capture her attention once again.

"I wouldn't mind doing a dry run of the full song with you and my band when they arrive mid-day tomorrow."

"What time?" She fiddled with her fork without looking up. "I'll be back on the clock."

Yeah, well, I'm pretty tight with your boss. Getting her off the clock wouldn't be any problem. "Not sure yet. It depends on when the rest of The Texans arrive." On a burst of boldness, he asked, "Mind giving me your number, and I'll text you when we're ready to get started?"

This time she did look up, and her expression was bleak. "I'll be around. Just have the front desk page me." She abruptly stood.

Out of politeness, he stood as well, but she was already walking determinedly away.

He stared after her, wondering what in the heck he'd done wrong. Again.

A light touch on his arm made him glance down. A younger, very pregnant version of Shiloh Neeson was staring up at him.

"Hi. I'm Shayley Neeson." She held out a pale, slender hand.

"Nice to meet you." He shook her hand, surprised at how swollen her fingers felt. "You must be Shiloh's sister."

"The one and only," she returned cheerfully, brushing her hand over her beach ball sized belly before dropping it to her side.

He didn't know what else to say, so he waited.

She continued in a soft voice that gave him the impression she didn't wish to be overheard by the others. "I came over here to tell you to be patient with her, okay?"

He spread his hands. "Is it always like this with her? One step forward, two steps back?"

Shayley chuckled despite her sober expression. "No. It didn't used to be like that at all. But this is the version of her that the Marines sent home to me. I've always thought that something must have happened over there — something that neither she nor my husband have been willing to talk about." She made a face and explained, "They served together overseas."

"I'm always sorry to hear about soldiers suffering."

Gabe probably understood it better than most. Like his job, folks tended to only see the glitz and glamour — or in their case, the welcome home parades and flag waving — not the sacrifices.

He angled his head at the silver door. "Care to go for a walk?" There was nothing he'd like more than to hear the rest of Shiloh Neeson's story.

"She can't."

Gabe glanced up in surprise at the dark, rugged cowboy whose approach he hadn't heard.

"Foster Kane." The guy stuck out a hand. "Shayley's brother-in-law. I'm about to take her home for a visit with my brother." He paused a beat before adding, "her husband."

It suddenly dawned on Gabe that Shiloh's sister must be married to the nut job who lived next door — the one Matt said was asking to pull security at the upcoming charity concert. It was more than a little odd that the guy was living apart from his pregnant wife. Gabe sensed there was more to the story.

He wasn't overly thrilled about having a known conspiracy theorist in charge of security, but he trusted his brother's judgment. Gabe usually kept a bodyguard or two on tap during concert performances, anyway, so he'd already have an extra level of insulation between him and any security threats.

He and Foster shook hands, taking each other's measure. Then Foster stepped back to splay a hand against Shayley's lower back. Gabe was struck by the possessive gesture. Apparently, he took his role as a brother-in-law seriously, maybe a little too seriously. It was almost as if he was trying to warn Gabe away or something.

Glancing up at Foster, Shayley continued speaking in a more shy voice than before. "I was just telling Gabe to be patient with our Shiloh. I know she comes across as tough as nails, but it's only because she's been through a lot."

"Don't worry, Shay. I'm keeping an eye on her." Foster's tone was flat.

Again, Gabe had the distinct impression that Foster was warning him to keep his distance.

"I know you are." Shayley's expression softened with adoration as she searched his face. "But tonight was good for her. She really needed this." Her gaze flitted back to Gabe. "Hearing her sing tonight was like getting a piece of her back that I was starting to think was gone forever."

Wow! Gabe was rendered speechless again. He was truly honored by the part he'd played in that, however small. However, there was still the matter of ensuring Shiloh Neeson would be present at his band practice mid-day tomorrow.

"So, ah..." He eyed Foster speculatively, hoping the guy wouldn't think he was crossing a line. "Shiloh agreed to a dry run with my band tomorrow, but I'm not a hundred percent sure when they'll arrive. What's the best way to get ahold of her when they do?"

"Me," Shayley said simply. She reached inside the

pocket of her black leggings and withdrew a phone. "She and I are supposed to be sharing a cell phone, but she mostly leaves it with me. What's your number? I'll text you to get a conversation thread going." Then she gave a snorting laugh and glanced up from her typing. "Oh, sheesh! Did I really just ask for Gabe Romero's number like it was no big deal? *The* Gabe Romero?"

"Stop already." Grinning, he shook his head at her and started reciting his number. She continued to snicker as she typed. A few seconds later, the phone in his pocket vibrated with an incoming message.

"There you go, Mr. Famous Singer Guy. Now you can summon my sister's bee-you-tee-ful voice anytime you need it."

"Thanks." He winked, eliciting another chuckle from her and a scowl from Foster.

"We gotta go, Shay." Foster nodded at the door. "It's getting late, and Samson's waiting for us."

———

Even though it was after dark when Gabe returned to his room, he opened his window again. He knew the chances were slim, but he was already dying to hear Shiloh's phenomenal voice again. Though she was standoffish and hadn't exactly shown any interest in getting to know him better on a personal level, she was all he could think about tonight.

It was silent outside. The bay of cattle had

muted, the moon had risen to a full white glow, and thousands of stars were studding the skies. His mind drifted back to the song he and Shiloh had sung together. Inevitably, he relived the way he'd felt when he'd sung while gazing directly into her eyes.

He'd read sadness there and mystery, fear intermingled with hope. She was a snarl of too many emotions to name them all, but there'd been interest there, as well. She'd noticed him as a man, and she'd liked what she'd seen. Only while they were singing, though. Afterward, she'd masked her feelings all too quickly. No, she'd done more than that. She'd shut down his only attempt at starting a conversation and had all but run from the room.

Still...

Gabe turned away from the window, longing to know more about the lovely ex-Marine. Whether she intended to or not — and he was leaning toward not — she'd utterly captured his attention. There'd been a connection between them, if only for a short period of time, one he could still feel.

Even now, the mystery in her eyes was making musical notes dance around in his head. New notes. New words. New feelings. New inspiration.

"Ah, what the heck?" After a moment of deliberation, he gave in to the temptation to turn his keyboard on. Sitting down on his black swivel stool, he opened his notebook and plunked out the keys to the music swimming around in his head. *Yeah, baby! I like it.* Running both hands over the keyboard, he found his groove and started to play.

Every few seconds or so, he stopped to write in his notebook. He owned a special program that would allow the keys he was playing on his keyboard to appear directly on his computer screen, but sometimes he preferred to go old-school and compose one note and word at a time.

Tonight was one of those times. Maybe tomorrow he would add in the extra runs and chords with the help of his program. But, for now, he just needed the melody playing inside his head to find its way onto paper.

He fiddled with the keys and sang far into the night, unable to recall the last time he'd felt this inspired. The walls of discouragement that had been blocking his creative process in recent weeks were gone. The music flowed freely from his heart, to his hands, to his notebook.

The result was a song called *Soldier Girl.* It was about a girl who'd gone off to war and the boy she'd left behind, who'd wished every night on the same star she was sleeping under to come safely home to him.

It was past two o'clock in the morning when Gabe finally shut off his keyboard. The song he'd written probably wasn't one he'd ever share publicly. It was too close to home. However, he already had the start of another two songs bouncing around in his head. Before he fell into bed, he took an extra minute to write his ideas in his black notebook, so he could revisit them in the morning.

A flutter of wings made him glance at the window. *Shoot!* He'd left it open, and the biggest moth he'd ever seen was ramming repeatedly against the screen, trying valiantly to reach the small desk light he had suspended over his keyboard.

Thank goodness for window screens! Otherwise, who knew how many critters would be flying around his room by now? With a silent chuckle, he moved across the room to shut the window. But before he lowered it completely and latched it, he paused one last time to listen for Shiloh's voice — just in case.

Nothing more than the drone of tree frogs droned around his ears.

———

Shiloh didn't sleep much that night. Long after the lights were turned out, a certain pair of dreamy dark eyes continued to gaze into her soul, the same way he'd looked at her while they were singing together earlier.

What do you want from me, Gabe Romero? Though Shiloh was too honest with herself to pretend there was no attraction sizzling between them, she knew better than to read too much into it. He was a celebrity country singer; she was a maid. He was rich; she was poor. He would be leaving town again soon; she had no plans to leave her sister's side. At least not until she'd safely delivered her baby and had a chance to rest, recover, and get back on her feet.

And not until Shiloh could be certain that the danger that had followed her home from Afghanistan was gone for good. She'd managed to acquire a secret admirer of sorts. A man who'd started sending her strange text messages while she was still recuperating from her battle wounds in the hospital – messages that were more disturbing than romantic. They usually ran no more than three to four words and pretty much said the same thing over and over again.

You are mine.

I made you mine.

Together again soon.

I'm coming for you.

Forever mine.

The strange text messages, with their threatening overtones, were the primary reason she'd accepted Samson Kane's invitation to move her and her sister off the grid with him and his friends, following the death of their father. Samson was far from perfect, but their near isolation from the rest of the world while living on his military-esque compound had finally put a stop to the stalky messages. It probably helped that she'd given up her old cell phone and number during that time, so Mr. Unrequited Love had no way of reaching her.

And she preferred to keep things that way.

To continue keeping a low profile.

To be a difficult target.

Sighing heavily, she turned to her side, fluffing her pillow before she laid her head back down. Sleep still continued to evade her, and it was just as well. Anytime she fell asleep, the nightmares came raging out of the cage where she kept them during the day.

Instead, she rested with her eyes open, like she had so many times while she was deployed overseas. Her thoughts inevitably returned to Kandahar. She still didn't remember much about what had happened that fateful afternoon. She'd been told that their camp had been ambushed. Two of her comrades had perished, and Samson had suffered severe burns while carrying her away from the ensuing explosion. But that exact sequence of events didn't match the horrors unfolding in her nightmares each night.

Time and time again, a different face than Samson's arose in her mind, the face of another soldier she didn't recognize. A man who was somehow part of the fire and the explosion that had ensued...*afterward*.

She abruptly sat up in bed. It was odd how it had never occurred to her until just now, but she was suddenly certain that the fire had come before the explosion — not the other way around, as she'd been told. Then her shoulders fell. Did it even matter? She'd gone to counseling a few times when she first returned to the States, and her therapist had explained that dreams — or nightmares, in her case — were often the result of trauma. To get rid of them, the woman had advised, Shiloh needed to come up with a new ending to it. She needed to rehearse the new ending inside her head both throughout the day and right before she went to bed at night.

The problem with that theory was that rehearsing fiction wasn't going to remove the scar from her face or reinstate her position as a soldier in the Marines. So she'd never really seen the point in playing games inside her own head.

Suddenly needing more air, Shiloh climbed out of bed and tiptoed barefoot to the window. Raising it, she climbed into the overstuffed chair beside it, snuggling closer to the fresh breeze whistling through the screen.

That was when she heard his voice.

Gabe Romero was singing again. He wasn't too far away, either, maybe only a room or two down from where she and Shayley were staying. It was difficult to hear his exact words, but the music was lovely. The way he kept pausing, then coming back to repeat the same notes, made her realize she'd caught him in the middle of composing.

Wo-o-o-ow! It was better than a backstage pass to sit there listening to him — like hearing genius in action. It wasn't as if she stood any real chance of going back to sleep, anyway. She closed her eyes, allowing Gabe's voice and the muted sounds of his electronic keyboard to soothe and transport her to a happier place, away from the fragments of her darkest memories.

Away from the man in the shadows who claimed she would forever be his, after he'd marked her by fire. *Wait!* Where had that thought come from? Her hand flew to her cheek in the moonlight, and her finger traced the ridges of her scar for the thousandth time. *He did this to me. He marked me.* She didn't know how she knew it. She just did. Her throat tightened.

She'd long since accepted the fact that her face was damaged, but it had never occurred to her that the damage might have been deliberate. *Does it mean I'm finally remembering that day?* Or was it just another one of the many horrors rising from her nightmares?

On a whim, she stood and padded her way to the vanity. Turning on the light over the sink, she squinted for a moment against the sudden burst of brightness until her eyes became accustomed to it. Then she leaned closer to the mirror to examine her scar more closely. Seconds later, she sighed in relief. There was no sign of a message in the jagged scar. No letters or pictures. The only part of her scar that remotely resembled anything was the widest part of the scar just below her cheekbone. If she used a dose of imagination, she could just barely make out the head of an arrow pointing west. She leaned closer to the mirror, wondering if she was seeing things that weren't there. People saw pictures in the clouds every day, too, but a lot of that was simply wishful thinking on their part.

An arrow pointing west, though? For some reason, the thought made Shiloh shiver. Either that, or it was the breeze from the open window chilling her. Since Gabe had finally stopped singing, she tiptoed across the room to shut it. Then she lay back down in her bed and attempted to go to sleep. Each time she got close to drifting off, though, a voice in her head cried, *Mine, mine, mine! Always mine!*

Yeah, she wasn't getting any sleep tonight.

———

Gabe was a bit on the drowsy side from how late he'd worked, but he threw off his patchwork quilt the next morning with more excitement than he'd felt in a long time. Today he was getting to sing with Shiloh Neeson again.

Singing the words to *Soldier Girl* beneath his breath, he tossed on a simple navy t-shirt and yanked on a pair of jeans. Yesterday, he'd wanted to look like a country singer over dinner. Today, he simply wanted to come across as a regular guy, to not do anything that would rattle Shiloh or scare her away.

Sure, he'd found above-average success on the country music circuit, but most days he was just plain old flesh and blood like any other guy. A guy who was attracted to a beautiful, fascinating woman. A guy who longed to be more to her than an icon on a music poster. Singing with her last night had been a good start in that direction. He hoped to capitalize on that today.

His band arrived in a flurry of jokes, laughter, and

bulky equipment that they quickly assembled on stage. He waited until the musical instruments were in place and the sound checks made before texting Shayley.

Mind letting Shiloh know we're ready to get started?

Her response came back in seconds. *NP*

He smiled, understanding it was shorthand for "no problem."

Despite the fact that Shiloh worked in the same building where Gabe and his crew were setting up for the concert, it was a full ten minutes before she made her appearance.

"You called?" she inquired curtly. Though she was back in her usual plaid shirt and jeans, he noted that her hair remained unbraided. Her long blonde waves swung enticingly against her slender shoulders.

"Yeah. We're ready to run through our song." Upon a closer look, he could see the smudges of shadows beneath her eyes that probably matched his own. It looked as if she hadn't slept any more than he had, and he foolishly hoped it had something to do with her thinking and dreaming about him.

"Fine. Let's get started." Instead of joining him on center stage, she hitched herself up to sit on the edge of the stage with her legs dangling.

Okay, then. She clearly wasn't interested in small talk. He could handle that. Giving his curious band members a slight headshake, he marched to one of the microphone stands to remove a hand-held mike. Then he grabbed his main mike. Striding back in her direction, he plopped down beside her and handed over the secondary one.

"You ready?" he propped one booted leg up between them, making it easier to angle his body in her direction.

She nodded instead of answering.

He raised a hand to signal to his band. They obediently ran through the desired opening notes, and he started to sing.

To his delight, Shiloh listened to the first few lines like she had the night before. She seemed to have a natural ability to know that the song needed time to build in intensity. At just the right part — two lines from the end of the first verse — she joined her voice with his.

He possessed a powerful lead tenor, so her throaty alto provided the perfect blend. Though they'd never discussed the exact notes she should sing, she found them, effortlessly harmonizing with him as if they'd been singing together for years.

He adored the way her gaze instinctively settled on his, knowing it was probably her way of watching him for cues. Regardless of her reasons, it was exactly the way he wanted to sing with her. The only way.

Gazes locked, they reached the bridge of the song. He held up one finger to her, then pointed at his chest.

She gave the slightest of nods, immediately understanding that he wanted to sing it solo the first time through. On the second time, she blended her voice with his again, easily picking out her alto part. It was beautiful, yet suddenly not enough for Gabe.

Sensing that his band members were enjoying what they were hearing and knowing that their audience tomorrow night was also going to want more, he abruptly signaled for the music to stop playing.

Shiloh looked surprised and a little worried, as if fearing she'd done something wrong.

"I think we should take it from the top again. First verse solo, breaking into parts on the last two lines. On the second verse, I'd like us to switch parts. You sing it solo, and I'll join in on the last two lines."

Her rosy lips parted in silent protest, but he simply rushed ahead to finish the sequence he'd already envisioned. "I'll solo the bridge on our first run-through. Second time, we'll sing it in unison. The third time in parts." He made a rally sign in the air, the signal for his band to strike the opening notes again. "Folks are coming to the concert with their checkbooks out. I'd like for us to give 'em their money's worth."

To his relief, Shiloh didn't balk at his request. She simply followed the plan he laid out, and the result was the most satisfying sound of his career. Their voices rang across the renovated barn B&B, at times crooning and sighing, at other times crescendoing toward the climactic parts. They ended on a mellow note that didn't just resound throughout the room; it resounded inside of him.

Just like the night before, he got to watch Shiloh

lose herself in the beauty of the music. Her eyes grew distant and dreamy. Her expression was animated and utterly engrossed.

It was like his soul was singing directly to her, and hers was singing directly to him. The music they made together was both invigorating and inspiring. It was the biggest emotional high he'd ever experienced.

And for the first time in years, Gabe no longer felt alone.

CHAPTER 4: COMPETITION

Shiloh

Shiloh's breathing was shallow by the time she and Gabe finished the song. The Texans on stage behind them hooted and hollered with enough energy to raise the dead. A couple of the B&B guests had stepped into the dining area to listen, and they were clapping as well.

"Now *that's* country music!" the lead guitarist cried, strumming an extra ditty for emphasis. "Nice going, ma'am!" He was a wiry fellow with longish black hair dragging the collar of his shirt. An evening shadow added an air of ruggedness to his handsome features.

"Thanks." She felt her cheeks warm beneath his unfettered admiration. A part of her felt like weeping, too. It had been a long time since she'd felt so connected to anyone or anything the way she was to Gabe and his music. There was compatibility between them. Chemistry, even. And she had no flipping idea what to do about it. Her first instinct was to claim she had work piling up at the B&B and make her escape as quickly as possible.

But that wasn't true. Shayley had risen with an extra bounce in her step this morning and insisted that she felt well enough to handle the one room cleaning that needed to happen today. Plus, Shiloh wasn't a coward. She'd always prided herself on meeting challenges head-on. Why should her interaction with Gabe Romero be any different?

She forced herself to meet his dark gaze and felt her knees go weak at the pure male appreciation she saw there.

"Not gonna lie," he drawled, giving her a smug smile. "Normally, I run solo on gigs like this, but we sound good together."

"We do," she agreed, silently willing the flutter in her heart to subside. Gosh, but he filled out his navy t-shirt in all the right places. The guy either had a good gym membership or an incredible home workout regimen.

He rose to a crouch on the stage so he could go down on one knee in front of her. "Shiloh Neeson, will you make me the happiest country singer in Texas and open tomorrow's concert with me?" He held out one hand beseechingly to mimic holding a ring box.

His wedding-like proposal made her heart race. It also released a bubble of laughter from deep inside her. "I already said yes, you nut!" She playfully swatted his hand away.

He pressed both hands mockingly to his chest as he stood. "She said yes!" he crowed to no one in particular. Then he reached down to assist her to her feet.

Shiloh had spent so long taking care of herself and others, that she honestly couldn't remember the last time anyone had lent her a hand. As she curled her fingers against his longer ones and allowed him to tug her upright, the sweetest of sensations swept through her. This was what it would feel like to have someone in her life who cared.

He didn't immediately relinquish her fingers. "So, ah...we've gotta run through the rest of my songs. Any chance you'll stay to listen and critique?"

"Me critique *you?*" It was clear he was flirting. Pretending to be shocked, she withdrew her hand from his and clapped it over her mouth. "Have you forgotten what I do for a living?"

He arched a challenging brow at her. "I'm asking as one musician to another. That's all."

Sure you are. "I should probably warn you then." She shot him a teasing smile. "I'm already a big fan of The Texans. So if you want my critique, here it is. You guys sound amazing. All the time. End of story."

"I like her," his guitar player chortled. "You keep her around, and she'll give us all the big head."

Gabe purposefully turned his back on him. "If you stick around for practice, I promise to feed you lunch. My way of saying thank you for joining forces with me on stage."

On stage. Right. The reminder that she would be on display with him beneath the spotlights tomorrow made her inwardly cringe. "About being on stage with you," she murmured, glancing away, "I was hoping maybe you could keep the brightest lights off of this." She pointed at her scarred cheek. "There's only so much you can do with makeup." It was a good excuse, one he wasn't likely to question, but it wasn't her real reason for wanting to be out of the limelight. She quite simply didn't want any publicity that might bring her stalker scrambling out of the woodwork, assuming he was still alive and kicking.

"Not true," Gabe countered, looking appropriately concerned. "My makeup artist can turn you into an alien or one of Santa's elves with a few snaps of her fingers, and I'm happy to lend her services to you tomorrow. But if it's the lights you still want adjusted, I can make that happen, too."

"Yes, please," she begged softly. "I'd like to take you up on both offers, if it's not too much to ask."

"Done." He grinned in pleasure. "So, are we on for lunch today?"

"I think so."

"Bonus!" Still smiling, he strode back to center stage, leaving her standing where she was.

Facing his band, he announced, "I'd like to run through the rest of our concert songs from the top, focusing mainly on the transitions. Jay, I still have you on your big honking guitar solo before the bridge on song three. Mitch," he turned to his drummer, a sandy blonde hippie with his hair pulled back in a ponytail, "don't forget that jungle beat we discussed adding to song four. I want a steady offbeat during the first two verses, a nice build before the chorus, and then give it all you've got until the bridge. Then we'll step it back to the jungle again. Are we cool?"

His keyboardist waved two fingers. "Gotta question about the outro between songs one and two."

Gabe pointed his finger and thumb like a pistol. "Go ahead and shoot."

"What's the rhythm change again? I seem to remember you saying you wanted to switch it up next time."

"I do." Gabe snapped his fingers. "Thanks for the reminder." He swiveled around to his soundboard and punched a few buttons on the laptop that was connected to the controls. "Looks like we're at one hundred and thirty beats per minute on the first song. Let's go half-time on the second song to give our listeners more variety. Oh, and Mitch?" He glanced up at his drummer again. "I want you to stress the upbeat on that one."

"Got it." Mitch waved his drum sticks in affirmation.

Shiloh drank in all the musical jargon flying back and forth between the band members, thrilled to be immersed in the world of music. Gabe was truly the luckiest guy in the universe to have made a career out of something he loved so much.

Unlike me. She bit her lower lip. *A not-so-lucky gal.* There weren't many things less exciting than making beds and scrubbing toilets for a living. It was temporary, of course. *Or so I hope.*

She crept quietly down the platform stairs and made her way to one of the round tables resting directly below the stage. Pulling out a chair, she perched on the edge of it and prepared to be amazed all over again by The Texans.

Gabe didn't disappoint. Once he and his band finished talking through the changes he was making to a few songs, he launched right back into singing. And like he'd done last night and this morning, he sang directly to her, crooning his heart out through the microphone.

Shiloh knew she should probably go check on her sister. She should also probably pay a visit to the kitchen to see if Bree needed help with anything. And poor Harley, who'd been stuck at the check-in booth for the better part of two days, would've probably really appreciated a break. However, Shiloh couldn't bring herself to ditch Gabe, after he'd issued such a kind invitation to linger for the rest of practice and join him for lunch afterward.

She lost track of time as he sang and jolted in surprise when a large hand clapped down on her shoulder.

"I've been looking all over for you." Foster's voice

in her ear made her stiffen. "Thought you'd be done singing eons ago." His shirt and jeans were coated in a layer of dust, and his boots were caked with dirt. Even his Stetson, that had once been black, was now a dusty brown.

Shiloh glanced up at him, straightening in her seat. "Is Shayley okay?" she mouthed hastily, trying not to bemoan the extra work he was creating for her by tracking so much dirt inside the B&B.

"Yeah," he mouthed back, glancing in irritation at the stage. The Texans were still drenching the dining room with lights and sound. Angling his head at the front entrance, he beckoned her to follow him outside, presumably where it would be quieter so they could speak.

Shooting an apologetic look in Gabe's direction, Shiloh was surprised to see the country singer's face harden — not at her, but at Foster. It wasn't a friendly look, making her wonder if the two men had been involved in a previous argument or something. Biting back a sigh, she stood and followed Foster out the front double doors.

Foster rounded on her the moment they stepped outside. "What are you doing, Shy?"

"What do you mean?" she scowled at him, wondering why he was in such a crabby mood on such a beautiful day. The sun was rising to a full blast overhead. Wildflowers were blooming in riotous patches of color across the surrounding pastures where the cattle were grazing. Even the usual bluster of canyon breezes was toned down to a gentler cadence.

He clenched his fists. "Encouraging a guy like Gabe Romero is a very bad idea. Trust me."

"Oh, bug off already!" She turned back toward the shiny glass doors of the B&B with a sound of disgust. "I can't believe you called me out here for something so dumb."

"I was only trying to warn you. All of this talk about putting you on stage is hardly fair, considering..." He glanced away awkwardly, voice dwindling.

"Do you really think I care what people think about my scar?" she groused. She did, of course, but he didn't need to know that. He just needed to back off. It was bad enough that he was forever hovering over her sister; she didn't plan to allow him to do the same to her.

"You don't need the paparazzi breathing down your neck, Marine. Trust me."

There was something so low and menacing in Foster's tone that she spun back in his direction. "Well, I'd prefer not to have anyone breathing down my neck, including you."

"I'm not doing it because I want to." He jutted his chin at her. "I'm just trying to look after you and Shay."

She slapped at the air. "Like Shayley told you yesterday, we're not your responsibility, slick. I can take care of myself."

"Oh, really?" He lowered his dusty head to get

nose-to-nose with her. "Because Samson has a pretty different story to tell. In case you've forgotten, most of his scars are from carrying your skinny little hide away from that maniac and his twisted —" At her shocked expression, he broke off whatever else he was about to say.

A wave of dizziness shook her at the realization that Foster Kane might actually know more about the horrid ambush overseas than she did.

"Hey, are you okay?" He worriedly reached for her shoulders.

She sidestepped his attempt to steady her and ended up stumbling. Doing a stutter step to regain her balance, she demanded, "What did Samson tell you about the explosion?" He'd never said much to her about it, and she always figured it was because he had no more desire to revisit the ugliness of that day than she did.

Foster shook his head so vehemently that he knocked his Stetson askew. "No way. I've already said more than I should. Samson will toss me off the nearest canyon if he finds out."

Smiling without mirth, Shiloh advanced on him, giving her knuckles a threatening pop. "Samson is the least of your worries right now, buddy. You can either tell me what you know, or you'll be getting a first-hand lesson on how many pain receptors there are in the human body."

"Or we could just talk about it," he joked, eyeing her with extreme caution.

"Nah. I'm more of a show-and-tell kinda gal." Quick as a flash, she reached for his hand and twisted his thumb back.

"Ouch!" The moment he tried to pull it back, she applied more pressure.

"Two hundred pain receptors for every square centimeter on your sorry body," she taunted. "That means there are literally thousands of ways for me to cause you pain, if you don't tell me what I want to know."

Foster's upper lip curled. "You're a real brat, you know that?"

She pressed his thumb harder.

"Fine," he panted. "I'll choose being tossed off a canyon any day over..." He glanced down at his painfully extended thumb. "Whatever this is."

"Huh-uh." She narrowed her gaze on him. "First you talk; then I'll let you go."

"It was a fire that caused the explosion, not the other way around."

"I already knew that," she snapped, though her gut tightened sickeningly to have her suspicions confirmed. "What else?"

His mouth twisted. "Samson said a new soldier got transferred into your company right before it happened. Different squad than yours. He caught him staring at you in a way he didn't like. When he finally had the time to confront the guy, he found him messing with a cigarette lighter near the explosives. The guy swore he was just sneaking a smoke, but

Samson said his story felt off. The next thing he knew, the only female tent in the entire camp was on fire."

"Mine." Shiloh released Foster's hand as more snippets of her memories came flooding back. "My two roomies had just headed outside with their weapons on a trip to the latrine and I..." She paused as her vision blurred. "I was so exhausted that I decided to catch a few Z's before we broke camp and hit the road again." That was where her memories grew fuzzy, and her nightmares began each night.

"Samson thinks it was that same soldier who started the fire, and that the fire spread to the explosives."

"So there was no ambush?" she inquired weakly.

"Not the kind you would assume when you hear the word used."

"Meaning what, exactly?" She swayed on her feet, dreading what Foster was about to say next.

"That maniac attacked you, Shy. He came into your tent when you were sleeping with a makeshift branding iron in hand. And he—"

With a wounded sound, she clapped a hand to her scarred cheek.

"I'm sorry, Shy." Foster's face had gone pale. "I really am."

"Keep talking," she ordered shakily. "How did Samson find me?" *And why am I just now hearing about this?*

He shrugged. "You know how Sam is. A bit of a

lunatic at times, but he'll do anything for the folks he cares about. Said he sprinted for your tent the moment he saw the fire. He arrived just in time to catch that monster carving up your face and screaming that you belonged to him now. Sam fought the guy off of you, but he got away when the munitions outside caught fire. Then all hell broke loose."

Shiloh could piece together the rest of the story from there. Samson had run with her in his arms through the fire and subsequent explosions to get her to safer ground, incurring multiple serious injuries in the process.

"What happened to the creep who did this to my face?" she grated out.

Foster shook his head. "Samson reported what he knew to the authorities, but they never took him seriously. Said he had a distorted view of what had happened due to a traumatic brain injury. As soon as he got out of the hospital, he tried tracking down the guy on his own, only to find his name on a deceased list."

"I'm not so sure my attacker died that night, after all." Shiloh spoke through numb lips, wondering what the strange buzzing sound was in her ears. *Because that wouldn't explain how he tracked me down and started sending all those warped messages, particularly the one about how he "made me his."*

"Samson says the same thing. That's why he offered you and Shay a place on the compound after he found out about your stalker and all those weirdo texts you were getting from him. His working theory is that the guy might've faked his death by switching dog tags with one of the stiffs who actually died in the fire. Who knows?"

"The guy," she muttered slowly. "You keep calling him the guy, but Samson must have seen his real name on the deceased list, right?"

"It's Arrow, of all things." He shook his head in disgust. "His name is Arrow. Arrow Westfield."

Mercy! It all made sense now. Arrow Westfield had claimed over and over that she was his now, because he'd made her his. *By the arrow he carved on my face, pointing west.* The buzzing sound in Shiloh's ears grew louder. Then she slumped forward.

The last thing she heard was Foster frantically calling her name. Then everything went black.

———

She awoke to the strong scent of coffee. "Where am I?" she groaned, trying to sit up. One second she'd been arguing with Foster outside the B&B, and the next minute she'd... Her eyelids popped open in alarm as the memory of what Foster had revealed came flooding back.

"Where's Samson?" She glanced wildly around her, surprised to find herself on the floor of the kitchen. "We need to talk!" She wanted to know why he'd kept so much information about her stalker from her for so long. Was it because of his over-the-top paranoia or for some other reason? She also wanted to know anything and everything else he knew about the crazy creep named Arrow, or whatever he was calling himself these days.

Foster's face swam into view. The usual twinkle in his dark eyes was missing. In its place was raw concern. "Samson is where he always is."

"Well, I need to see him. Now!"

"And I'll take you to him," he promised, "just as soon as you assure me you're okay. Are you okay?"

"What do you think?" She rolled her eyes. Mindful of the fact that there were others in the room with them, she fibbed, "I was inside where it was deliciously cool, enjoying an amazing concert when you insisted on dragging me outside in that insane heat. All your mumbo jumbo about the baby could've seriously waited until after lunch." The lunch she was supposed to be attending with Gabe. *Ugh!* She sure hoped her quickie blackout hadn't blown her chances to share a meal with him.

Foster's brown eyebrows shot upward at the realization that she was fibbing about the topic they'd actually been discussing. "I, ah...right. I'm sorry," he muttered. "Guess I wasn't thinking."

"You seriously passed out from the heat?" Bree squatted down beside her, holding out a mug of coffee. Concern was stamped all over her lovely features.

To Shiloh's amusement, the ranch manager's wife was wearing cutoff jean shorts and a red and white checkered top that was tied around her middle, leaving an inch or two of her flawlessly tanned midriff bare.

"Actually, I think I locked my knees after that joker kept me standing for so long." Shiloh chuckled as she reached for the mug of coffee. "Gimme a sip of that famous brew of yours, Daisy Duke. It's the best pick-me-up in the world, which I could really use before my lunch date."

"Oo, a lunch date!" Bree smiled at Shiloh's reference to the Dukes of Hazzard show and handed the mug over. "Details, sister!"

"There are none." Shiloh made a face as she took a sip. "For all I know, I already missed it."

"Nope. We're still on for lunch, if you feel up to it." Gabe Romero's quiet baritone resounded across the room.

Foster visibly bristled. "Relax, man!" He glanced over his shoulder to watch Gabe's approach. "The girl just passed out. I was thinking of taking her to the hospital."

"You and what army, mister?" The smile Shiloh drenched him with was pure evil.

Though he edged away from her, he continued glaring at Gabe. "Regardless, the last thing she needs right now is to be dragged around town."

"Our lunch date is here at the B&B, actually," Gabe informed him coolly. "Bree's got a table for two set up for us on the back balcony."

Oh, wow! "Sounds wonderful to me." Despite

Foster's growling, Shiloh stood and faced Gabe, though her knees still felt a bit shaky. "I can't remember the last time I ate. It's entirely possible I collapsed from sheer malnourishment." She threw a ferocious scowl over her shoulder at Foster, daring him to contradict her.

He raised his hands in surrender and stepped back. "By all means, Marine. Go get nourished." There was a snide edge to his voice as he met Gabe's eye again.

As Gabe escorted Shiloh across the dimly lit dining room to the much brighter balcony outside, he slung an arm around her shoulders.

She couldn't immediately tell if he was being romantic, or if he thought she needed the support after what had just happened to her. Regardless of his reasons, her heart did a series of crazy little cartwheels in response. He was taller and rangier than his brother, Matt, but she quickly discovered he was just as solid.

When he led her outside on the balcony, she was enchanted to find a table brimming with wildflowers waiting for them. To her surprise, he didn't immediately hold out her chair to be seated. Instead, he walked with her to a white Adirondack two-seater by the railing. It was piled invitingly with red and blue striped throw pillows.

"How about we start off here?" He waved her onto the bench. "At least until Bree has a chance to deliver our lunch."

She gratefully took a seat on the contoured bench and tipped her head back.

Gabe sat beside her and scooted closer. Resting his forearm on the top of the seat behind her, he frowned down at her. "Are you sure you don't need to see a doctor? I could have you there and back in two snaps, if you want to play it safe."

"I'm a Marine," she reminded him demurely. "We're made of tougher stuff."

"True, but you're still not invincible."

She pretended shock. "You're kidding! And all this time, I—"

"Aw, shut up." He reached over to flick the tip of her nose. "I guess I'm just trying to convince myself you're okay."

"Like I keep telling everyone, I'm fine. It was a false alarm." She wished she was in the position to tell him more, but she wasn't.

"Okay, so on to the next problem." He drew a deep breath. "I know it's probably too soon to be asking stuff like this, but what's the situation between you and Foster? Are you two a thing?"

Normally, she would have been put off by someone prying into her personal business, but it was clear Gabe was asking out of jealousy. "Not even." She smothered a chuckle. "He's not my type."

"So I'm not competing with him, eh?" The way Gabe was looking at her made her breathing turn shallow all over again.

"For what?" she asked breathlessly.

"For this." Gabe swooped in to brush his warm mouth against hers.

"No," she breathed against his lips. "It's not like that between us."

"Good." Gabe leaned in to capture her mouth again. His hand gingerly cupped her damaged cheek, turning her face more fully into his kiss.

He didn't stop to explore her scar; he didn't give any indication that he even felt its puckered ridges against the pads of his fingers. He simply held her like it didn't matter.

When he finally raised his head, she whispered, "We really shouldn't be doing this."

"Why?" He ran his thumb along the line of her chin.

"Because I have issues. Lots of them." *Issues I don't want to involve you in. Ever.*

"Yeah? So do I." He gazed deeply into her eyes. "I'm not sure how much you know about Matt and me, but we were raised in foster care. I ran away when I was sixteen and never even finished high school. I had to go the G.E.D. route a few years later when I decided to attend college."

Her eyes widened. She was both surprised and saddened to discover he'd endured such a dismal childhood. "Seems to me like you eventually found your way."

"It took a while." He briefly glanced away. "I lied about my age so I could sing in nightclubs and hope-fully get noticed by the talent scouts."

"I think you succeeded."

"Not because of my lying and hustling," he confessed in a voice husky with emotion. "By some miracle, it happened during a college concert."

"So you believe in stuff like that, huh?" she teased.

"What's that?" He looked surprised.

"God."

"I do now." He reached for her hand and laced his fingers through it.

A delicious weakness coursed through her limbs. "Are you sure about this, Gabe? All we did was sing a couple of songs together." She shot him a half-curious, half-worried look. "We're going to sing one more tomorrow, and then you'll be gone."

"Not for good." His fingers tightened over hers. "Not if you give me a reason to keep coming back, Shiloh Neeson."

Somewhere in the back of her mind, a thousand warning bells were going off about the wisdom and timing of things, but she ignored them. For just a few minutes, she wanted to know what it was like to be Cinderella. She could hardly believe she was on a date with a celebrity country singer, much less in his arms. He was every one of her wildest dreams come true.

Maybe he would leave Anderson Ranch tomorrow after the concert, and maybe she would never see him again, but at least they had today and tomorrow.

"I can give you right now, Gabe." She reached up to brush back the dark wave of hair that had fallen over his forehead. "That's all I have to offer." That's all either of them really had to offer. He hadn't denied the fact that he was leaving town again pretty quickly; and her own future was uncertain, at best.

"I'll take it." His voice was husky with emotion as he gathered her closer.

She rested her head against his shoulder, and together they gazed across the peaceful fields that stretched across the southern side of Anderson Ranch. It felt a little like the calm before the storm, but Shiloh stubbornly pushed away such thoughts.

She'd promised Gabe she would give him now, and she was a woman of her word.

CHAPTER 5: SECOND THOUGHTS

Gabe

Gabe hated it when his lunch date with Shiloh finally drew to a close. He'd seriously dragged it out for as long as he could.

She set down her near-empty glass of lemonade and stood. "Sorry to have to scoot, but I really do have a job to get back to."

"I know." He stood and reached for her again.

His heart thumped with joy when she stepped, without hesitation, into his arms. "Best first date ever," he muttered against her temple.

"Really? How many of them have you had?" She sounded more amused than alarmed by his slip of the tongue.

"Too many," he sighed, cuddling her closer. "I'd say I'm ending on a high note, though."

She snickered against his shoulder. "What's that supposed to mean?"

"That I'd very much like for this to be my last first date."

She tipped her head back so she could gaze up at him. "I promised you right now, Gabe."

He gazed down at her, caressing her with his eyes. "I think you know I want more than that."

Her expression turned sad. "And we're both old enough to realize we don't always get what we want."

Fear tightened his gut. "Is there someone else in your life?"

"Romantically? No. I wasn't kidding about those issues, though. As sweet and wonderful as you are, Gabe, I seriously doubt you want to take on that kind of trouble."

"I want to take you on, Shiloh. So whatever that entails..." He let the words dwindle between them.

She stretched to the toes of her boots to give him a quick peck on the lips. "Then this is me saving you from yourself." Though he wasn't nearly ready to let her go, she gently disengaged herself from his embrace. "Thanks for lunch, Gabe. It was truly amazing." She took a few steps back and fluttered her hand at him.

"That's it?" he spluttered, staring after her.

"I promised you now," she reminded in a cheerful voice, walking backward. "That was a good hour ago."

"What about the concert?" he protested.

She reached the door leading back inside and paused. "Chill. I'll be there."

"And after that?" he demanded, hardly believing

she was simply walking away from everything they'd just shared. From the most romantic lunch date of his life. From all their kisses. From him.

She shrugged and twisted the door handle. Then she stepped inside the B&B and was gone.

No way! Gabe's hands went to his head as he turned around and stared blindly at the distant canyons. He stood there for several minutes, just breathing through the pain and disappointment. Otherwise, he might've done something stupid, like throw their blasted lunch table over the balcony, flowers and all. Never in his life had he allowed any woman to climb so far beneath his skin. Shiloh Neeson was driving him out of his mind!

The door opened and closed behind him.

"So how was it?" Bree sang out.

Gabe listened for a moment to the clink of plates and glasses as she began to clear the table. Then he turned around to face her, hands still clenched over his head.

"Whoa!" Her hands stilled on the sides of her bus bucket. "That bad, huh?" Her blue gaze filled with concern as she scanned his features.

He slowly lowered his hands. "It was incredible, actually."

"Oh?" She looked moderately relieved.

"Yeah. I think I may be in love."

"Ah." She went back to bussing the table, carefully setting their plates and glasses inside her bucket. "I guess that explains the tortured look."

"Then she just ended it and walked away," he continued bitterly.

Bree frowned and paused her clearing again. "You mean, she broke up with you?"

"No, I—" He stopped and shook his head. "I didn't ask her out. Not officially, at least, but it was understood." He didn't know why he was confiding in his brother's wife like this. It's not like they knew each other very well. But she and Matt were seriously all the family he had, and he was desperate, so he kept talking. "I kissed her, and she kissed me back. More than once."

"Whoa! TMI." Bree chuckled, looking a little embarrassed.

Tough. You're here, and you're family, so suck it up. "Then she just walked away," he repeated. "Said she has issues that she's protecting me from."

Bree's blonde brows rose. "She does, Gabe. Both of those Neeson girls do. As sweet and pretty as they are, you probably dodged a bullet."

His heart sank. "I'm sorry you feel that way, because I think I've finally found a woman worth taking a bullet for." Gabe knew it was a foolish thing to say, but it was true. He'd never felt this way about any woman before, and he really didn't care how many issues Shiloh had. He couldn't just walk away from her the way she'd walked away from him. Not after singing with her, holding her, and kissing her. Oh, and composing a song about her last night.

Bree studied him in troubled silence. "Are you

sure about that, Gabe?" She made a face at him. "I mean, you're about to get back on the road right after the concert tomorrow, aren't you? No offense, but I'm sure Shiloh knows that. Maybe walking away was just her way of insulating her heart against the inevitable."

"I'll always come back," he muttered. "I tried to tell her that. I'll keep coming back so long as she keeps giving me a reason to."

Bree's smile was empathetic. "So you'll be gone a month," she repeated, "and back for what? Two or three days before taking off again?"

"Probably." He shrugged. "I'll stay longer if I can. It depends on my tour schedule."

"Are you listening to yourself?" She gave him a sad smile. "Because it sounds to me like you'll be gone a lot more than you'll be here. Don't you think it'll be hard to build a relationship on that?"

"So what are you saying?" he exploded. "That I should quit my career to date Shiloh Neeson?"

"Of course not." Bree wrinkled her nose at him. "Well, not completely. It's just that Shiloh has already lost so much. Her parents. Her home. Her military career. So if you're going to pursue a gal like her, she's going to need some assurances from you. Some constants. A guy she can count on. Not someone who's always coming and going."

He was aghast at how matter-of-fact Bree sounded. "Unless you know of any full-time gigs here in the Texas panhandle..." He paused. "Or at the

B&B, for that matter." Money wasn't an issue. He'd done well for himself the past several years, but music was all he knew. He didn't have a computer science degree like his brother or a background in the military, nor would he survive behind a desk at the ranch. The only thing he'd ever excelled at was holding a microphone. It was part of who he was, if not the biggest part.

"Gosh, I wish!" She chuckled. "Maybe someday, but that's beside the point. I'm just trying to say you might need to be in town a little more often if you're going to properly wine and dine your special lady."

"Or..." His mind raced. There was one other possibility, one that involved him talking Shiloh Neeson into going on the road with him. Not right now, of course. He doubted she'd be willing to leave her sister's side until after the baby was born, and he wouldn't ask her to. But after that? Well, anything was possible.

"Or what?" Bree asked curiously.

"Never mind. I was just thinking out loud." He shook his head. It was too soon to talk about his latest brainstorm. First, he had to convince Shiloh to trust him enough to date him. The attraction was clearly there, and it wasn't one-sided. She kissed him like a woman who cared. And he wasn't buying that walk-away stuff. She could pretend indifference all she wanted, but he was willing to bet big bucks that she was thinking about him right now. She was thinking about him and remembering their kisses the same way he was.

Bree returned to clearing the table. "Well, Matt and I are here any time you want to talk. That's what family's for. In case he hasn't told you, Matt's ecstatic to have you back in his life. We both are."

"Thanks...sis." On a burst of happiness at her words, he moved to the table to help her finish cleaning up after his and Shiloh's lunch date. He even lugged the bucket of soiled dishes back to the kitchen for her.

His band members were gathered around the bar where the staff took their meals, munching their way through a fresh batch of the Italian pizza Bree had served the night before.

Angling his head at Jay, Gabe silently beckoned him aside. His lead guitarist rose, still laughing at something Mitch had said. He gave their drummer and keyboardist a high-five as he made his way over to where Gabe was standing. "Boss is calling. Gotta run."

He swaggered up to Gabe. "Yo. Whatcha need?"

Gabe kept his voice low, preferring not to be overheard by Bree in the hopes that his plan wouldn't filter back to Shiloh too quickly. "Are you still dating that videographer?"

"Maybe." Jay's grin was cocky. "Any particular reason we're whispering?"

Gabe snorted. He wasn't whispering; he just wasn't talking at either of Jay's preferred decibel levels — loud and louder. "Any chance we can fly her into town tomorrow to record the charity concert?"

"I can ask. Are you, by any chance, offering to buy her a last-minute plane ticket?" Jay hooked his thumbs through his belt loops, looking expectant.

"Yep. I'll even upgrade her to first-class."

"Sweet!" Jay whipped out his cell phone and started texting. "I can tell you right now that her answer's going to be yes, no matter how much work it'll take to clear her schedule on such short notice."

"Oh, yeah?" Gabe was fascinated to note that Jay's girlfriend started texting back almost immediately. "Why's that?"

"Because she's been begging me to put in a good word with you for months. I can guarantee she's going to jump at the chance to work a project with you."

"Well, why didn't you say something before?" Gabe scowled at his friend.

Jay pushed his Stetson back farther on his head. "I didn't want you to feel obligated. Plus, I didn't need a female in my life who was only using me to get to you. If that's the case with Jolene, she's been really patient." He snickered as he read what his girlfriend had typed. "It's a big 10-4, chief. I won't bother reading you the whole gushing paragraph she sent. Short version is you just made my woman very happy."

"You're welcome."

"Is this something we need to keep on the down-low, boss?" Jay's voice was mocking.

"Only for a few days. The plan is to plaster snippets of the video recording across the band's social media accounts."

Jay nodded, still grinning. "I don't reckon this has anything to do with trying to impress our pretty little guest singer? Or, better yet, helping her get noticed by the talent scouts?"

When Gabe didn't answer, Jay whistled. "So that's the way the wind is blowing between the two of you. I was wondering."

"I don't pay you to wonder," Gabe pointed out dryly.

"Then you're getting it for free. I wish you all the luck in the world, Romeo. I really do."

Though Gabe appreciated his friend's sentiments, he wasn't so sure that mere luck was going to be enough.

———

To his intense disappointment, he didn't see much of Shiloh until the next evening when the time for the charity concert rolled around. Like they'd done for his previous visit, everyone on the Anderson Ranch staff pitched it to transform the B&B's steak restaurant into a dinner theater.

Bree had opted for a patriotic theme. There were alternating navy and white linen cloths draping the round tables, and she had the same porcelain cowboy boot vases on display as last time. This time, however, they were stuffed to overflowing with red geraniums.

"Looks like we're sold out!" Bree's brother, Brody, announced in satisfaction as he strolled through the dining room. Though he was no longer using the cane Gabe remembered, he still walked with a faint limp. Matt had mentioned something about him getting caught in a bull stampede some time ago. Thanks to some innovative physical therapy from one of Matt's former Army buddies, however, Brody was finally getting better.

Gabe gave Brody a double thumbs up at the news. "I'm really hoping this means we're going to raise some serious moolah."

Brody continued limping his way in Gabe's direction. "In case I forgot to say it, I really appreciate you doing this." He adjusted his Stetson lower on his tanned forehead. "As you may be aware, I fronted two of my newest staff members some money to cover their medical expenses, but it would've taken a really long time for them to pay me back...if ever. So this is a huge help to all of us."

Gabe shrugged, liking the guy's humble, grateful attitude. "Like I keep telling Matt, it's one of the perks of being family." He didn't mind the fact that he'd be raising money for Shiloh's younger sister's stint in the hospital before she came to work at the B&B. He even dared to hope it might earn him a few brownie points with her. It was a little less thrilling to be assisting Foster Kane with his medical bills, not that Gabe was in any way uncharitable minded. The guy just had the biggest chip on his shoulder.

Brody swung out a hand to Gabe. "We are enormously grateful. If there's ever anything we can do for you in return, here at the ranch, please don't hesitate to give me a holler." His lips twitched. "Like you already so well stated, it's one of the perks of being family."

Gabe felt a twinge of guilt at the reminder that Brody and Bree had utterly refused to let him pay for his room on the second floor of the B&B. "Thanks, man." As he shook Brody's hand, he caught sight of Shiloh out of the corner of his eye. She was on a ladder, stringing white lights across the dining room. Her simple black running shorts and white tank top indicated she'd probably gone on a run at some point earlier.

A peal of laughter escaped her as she reached down to accept a new string of lights from the man assisting her. He was none other than Foster Kane, wearing the same barn red shirt tucked into his jeans that all the other ranch hands had on. Apparently, it was their uniform of the day. Whatever he said made her wave her staple gun threateningly at him.

The easy camaraderie between them was unmistakable. So was the affection. Though they seemed to be forever scrapping over something, there was no denying they were close. Shiloh had claimed there was nothing romantic between the two of them, but Gabe had to wonder if the cowboy standing beneath her ladder had gotten that memo. It wasn't as if there was anything concrete between her and Gabe, either. She'd made it pretty clear that the kisses they'd shared yesterday were a onetime thing.

But not if I can help it! You'll be noticing me this afternoon, darling. I'll make sure of it. Nodding at Brody, Gabe tried to tamp down on his irritation as he jogged to the stage and mounted the stairs two at a time. He would've preferred to stop by Shiloh's ladder and invite her to join him on stage, but he had no interest in playing the jealous third wheel. He and The Texans would be making enough noise soon to get her attention.

His band members were going through their final sound checks when he stepped behind the curtain.

Jay had a teasing glint in his eyes. "Nice of you to show up."

"He's the big cheese. He's supposed to be fashionably late," Mitch mocked, twirling his drum sticks in the air before bringing them down in a quick, jazzy solo.

Gabe mimed a pitcher's wind-up and pretended to lob a baseball at his drummer. "That's it. I'm giving you an extra solo. The vocal kind."

"Ha!" Mitch looked unconcerned. "Only if you want to clear the building instead of fill it. My parents wouldn't even let me sing in the shower while growing up."

As the band members snickered, Gabe moved to the main microphone to test the backup batteries. There was a lull in their conversation, during which the sound of Shiloh's voice rang out across the dining room. She was practicing their opening song from the ladder where she was working.

Having zero interest in turning what he was about to do into another joking matter with the guys, Gabe moved determinedly in her direction. Whipping the stage curtains aside, he gazed at the woman he was quickly falling for, tickled to no end to find Foster had finally left the room. He watched her hum and sing for a few moments, utterly enchanted by her voice. Then he jogged down the stairs in her direction.

Moving to stand below her ladder, he reached up to hold the strand of lights she was stretching to tack into place with her staple gun. His assistance freed up one of her hands and made the process go much quicker.

"Thanks!" She reached for the next strand.

He assisted her with that one, too. Then, without warning, she started singing again. Unable to resist, he joined his voice with hers, letting his tenor and her alto intertwine as perfectly as they had before. Man, but the two of them sure made beautiful music together!

The only shadow on his happiness was the fact that she seemed to be trying to keep the scarred side of her face averted from him. Though the gesture troubled him, he didn't see any point in making an issue out of it. After they sang the final line of the song together, he purposefully moved directly into her line of sight, making it impossible for her to continue avoiding meeting his gaze.

"We should probably head on stage soon for a sound check." He searched her expression for affirmation. "Your voice is so mellow that I want to make sure I have the right volume in the mix."

She dropped her gaze. "Um, about that, Gabe..."

"About what, darling?" The endearment slipped out of him by accident, though he didn't mind her hearing it.

Her cheeks turned pink. "I really appreciate the way you invited me to join you on stage. I do."

You're canceling on me? Now?

Her long blonde lashes fluttered against her cheeks. "I'm just not sure if it's a good idea. Please don't be mad. I have my reasons. Good ones."

His frustration level edged up. It really wasn't a big deal in terms of the charity event itself. Their audience was coming to see him and The Texans. But it was a big deal to him personally. He wanted Shiloh on stage with him. He wanted her there so badly that disappointment was crashing through him at even the thought of her backing out.

"What are you afraid of, Shiloh?" he demanded hoarsely. "Me? Us?"

"No." Her smile was bittersweet, her voice sad.

"Last night I told you I think you're amazing. That hasn't changed."

"But you *are* afraid of something," he muttered bitterly. "Either that, or you don't trust me."

"Just let it go, please." Her expression was beseeching.

"I can't," he said simply. "I want you up there beside me this evening, Shiloh Neeson. I want it so badly that it's impossible to just shrug it off and walk away, the way you did yesterday."

"Wow! You're relentless," she murmured, toying with the last strand of lights.

"Where you're concerned, yes. My makeup artist is ready and waiting for you backstage. We'll adjust the lighting any way you want. I'm serious, Shiloh. I'll do whatever it takes to get you up there beside me."

He caught some movement from the corner of his eye and glanced up to see Brody Anderson striding in their direction.

"The lights look good, Shiloh. Real good." Brody gazed in approval around the room, rocking back on the heels of his boots. His hands were lightly tucked in the pockets of his jeans. "How about you let me put that ladder away for you while you go get changed?"

She scowled at him. "What is this? A premeditated, multi-frontal attack?" Glancing between the two men for a moment, she skipped down the rungs of her ladder. "Okay. I see how it is. This is me," she gave a mocking bow, "going to put on that ridiculously frilly white dress Bree insisted I wear. Then I'll be back to have an equally ridiculous amount of makeup slathered on. Are you two happy now?"

"Yes!" they chorused in unison.

She shook her head at them. "Did you practice that, too?" she inquired sweetly. Then she spun away from them. "Never mind. I don't really want to know the answer to that."

Brody shook his head at her retreating figure. "She's definitely a work-in-progress, but I like what I see in her."

So do I. Gabe stared after her helplessly, remembering her kisses and the way her strong, lithe arms had been entwined around his neck. He wanted nothing more than to run after her and pull her back into his arms to see if the magic they'd experienced last night was still there.

"She's by far one of the hardest working employees I've ever had on staff." Brody adjusted his brown leather vest over his red shirt. "I wish I had ten more of her."

I only want one. Gabe nodded without speaking, and Brody soon moved away to check on his other staff members.

————

To Gabe's intense relief, Shiloh ducked her head behind the stage curtains a mere twenty minutes later.

For a few seconds, he could only stare. The frilly dress she'd been crabbing about hugged her slender frame like a glove. The length of it cascaded down her toned legs, which were encased in cowgirl boots again. The hem dropped to just above her knees in front, though it fell nearly to the floor in the back. It was one of those trendy, asymmetrical dresses — probably intended to showcase her boots — and she looked incredible in it.

"You don't need any makeup, darling." The moment he spoke, Gabe wished he hadn't.

"Thanks, but I do." She pointed at the pink puckered skin on her cheek.

"That's not what I meant."

"I know, and it's really sweet of you, but I do need makeup. So point the way, Mr. Romero."

He promptly sent her backstage and continued his sound checks with the guys.

She returned only a handful of minutes later to the stage, making his jaw drop in astonishment. Her scar was gone. Well, probably not gone, but it was completely buried beneath her stage makeup.

"You weren't kidding," she announced with a chuckle. "Your makeup artist is a magician."

Uncaring that they had an audience, Gabe moved to stand in front of her. He tipped up her chin to examine her makeup more closely. "You are truly the most beautiful woman I've ever met, with or without makeup."

"I seriously doubt that." Her color deepened at

the compliment, though. She took a step back, and he dropped his hand.

"Thank you for doing this for me," he said softly.

She rolled her eyes. "It's not like you or Brody gave me much of a choice."

He pretended like he hadn't heard her crabbing. "Okay. Let's talk positioning, shall we?"

She shaded her eyes with her hands against the powerful spotlights. "This is the part where you keep your word and stick me somewhere in the background."

He would've much rather had her stand right next to him, but he nodded. Jay's girlfriend, Jolene, was already working her way around the room, setting up her cameras from the best angles possible. She could probably adjust the lighting in the video after the fact, if necessary. One way or the other, Gabe was determined to capture some footage of him and Shiloh singing together.

Yeah, Shiloh was probably aware there'd be cameras rolling while they sang together. Surely, she'd noticed Jolene setting them in position, while she'd been stringing lights for the past hour or so. However, Gabe couldn't help feeling a stab of guilt over the fact that he had a personal agenda for the video.

Then again, he'd always been a go-big-or-go-home kinda guy. He knew the video had the potential for making or breaking their relationship going forward. But, heck! The way he saw it, Shiloh had been backing away and running from him ever since they met. He really didn't have much to lose.

As the old saying went, *desperate times call for desperate measures*. And Gabe was growing desperate. He only had a few hours left to convince her to date him before he had to head back to the airport. It truly was now or never.

CHAPTER 6: GOING VIRAL

Shiloh

Shiloh caught her breath as the long, black stage curtains parted, revealing a dinner theater crammed full of guests. As Gabe had promised, his crew had her standing several steps behind him on the right, tucked securely in the shadows. The strobe lights rotated across the stage in glinting shafts of red, white, and blue. However, their beams always stopped just shy of her position.

The Texans erupted into the opening notes of their first song, with the twang of an electric guitar and bang of drums, that had their audience shooting to their feet.

Gabe grabbed the microphone and sang the first verse into it. Even though he was standing a good ten feet away, facing the auditorium, she sensed he was singing directly to her. It was real, and it was personal. Her heart was racing with anticipation by the time he reached the last two lines where she joined in.

Her voice came out much softer and breathier than usual. *Oh, sheesh! I'm so nervous!* Gabe's sound-board guy immediately turned up the volume of her mike to compensate for it.

Knowing her solo was coming up next, she drew on her military training to quell her nerves. *I can do this. I will do this.* She forced an even cadence to her breathing and launched into the second verse with more confidence. The audience craned to get a better look at her, but Gabe's lighting crew made no change to the strobes, keeping her out of the main spotlights as requested.

Thank you, Gabe. The tension in her shoulders eased as she continued to sing. *You kept your end of the deal; I'll keep mine.*

Gabe joined her on the last two lines in a riveting splash of harmony that elicited a rippling murmur of appreciation from their audience. A spontaneous smattering of clapping met their launch into the chorus, as they belted out the familiar tune of *Under the Texas Stars*, an all-time fan favorite.

"So many stars," they sang, "that I lose myself in them. Lose myself in love. Lose myself in you."

Though it wasn't part of what they'd practiced, Gabe turned his face sideways, making it clear to anyone who was watching closely enough that he was singing to Shiloh — to her, for her, and because of her. He poured all of his heart and energy into the music. Despite the number of times Shiloh had listened to his songs on the radio, she'd never heard him sing quite like this before. His voice was rich and alive, pulsing with emotion.

When they finished the song, the clapping and cheering went on for so long that Gabe signaled his band for an encore. Shiloh followed his cues and repeated the chorus and bridge with him, then sang through the chorus one last time. Before the last notes of music completely died and before Shiloh had taken the first step to leave the stage, Gabe launched into his second song.

Eep! Time for me to go. She felt a little off balance about the fact that they'd never gotten around to discussing her exit plan, which would've been nice. *Oh, well.* Edging her way toward the nearest exit, she was surprised to hear him singing a tune she'd only heard once before — the night she'd left her window open upstairs. At the time, she'd not been able to hear the words, but now she could.

"She's the girl on the sidewalk I met in eighth grade. She's the cheerleader who celebrated all the game points I made." It was a sweetly poignant melody with a mellow, swinging cadence.

The audience drew in a collective breath of surprise as they realized they were hearing something new from their favorite country music icon.

"She's the princess I took to the prom in the spring," he sang huskily. "She's the graduate I knelt for and offered a ring." It was slower than the last song, full of rich expression and heartfelt moments that nearly everyone in the room could relate to.

Shiloh stood riveted in the shadows of the sidelines, unable to finish walking away without first hearing the rest of the words.

Gabe moved straight into the second verse. "She's the girl who said yes to my hopes and my dreams. At our son's soccer games, she has the loudest screams. She's my hero in uniform who told me goodbye. She's the one I miss, my heart's deepest cry." Then the music changed, and the drums escalated to a more military sounding cadence before he launched into the chorus.

"She's my soldier girl, my heart unfurled, my entire world..."

Oh, Gabe! Shiloh pressed a shaking hand to her chest and squeezed her eyes shut, letting the music hold her in its enthrall and carry her away. Only when the dampness of tears slid down her cheeks, did she realize she was still standing on the outermost edge of the stage, just beyond the reach of the cameras.

Though her vision was blurred, it seemed to her that the audience was getting emotional, as well. Several people were dabbing at their eyes, and her sister was one of them. Gabe's lighting crew had turned their strobes on the audience for the song, bathing them in red, white, and blue flags that were rippling gently in a virtual breeze.

As if being pulled by a powerful, magnetic force,

Shiloh's gaze met and held Gabe's. And, at that moment, she fell in love with him.

It took her a moment to realize she was crying. Deep, heartfelt sobs fell silently from her lips as years of fear, uncertainty, and pain were stripped away. Every day she'd spent apart from her loved ones and every sacrifice she'd ever made suddenly seemed more worth it.

Because of the beautiful words of his song.

Because it meant he understood, on some level, all that she'd suffered.

Because he loved her in return.

Though the kaleidoscope of flags continued to sweep over the room, Shiloh's soldierly instincts kicked in the moment she noticed there were more than stage lights in play. The flicker of rotating red and blue ambulance lights flashed briefly through the double glass doors, then disappeared around the side of the B&B where the kitchen exit was located.

Oh! My! Lands! Wondering who'd become injured or ill, Shiloh pressed farther back into the shadows of stage right, finally dropping Gabe's gaze. She spun around and dashed past a few discarded stage props to reach the side exit leading outside.

She had to fist both hands in her skirts to lift the long back hem so she could run down the short flight of stairs without tripping. Sure enough, an ambulance was idling outside the kitchen. Blue-uniformed EMTs were bustling an empty stretcher through the side door to the kitchen.

Shiloh flew down the side of the building, fully planning on following the EMTs inside, but Crew Anderson stopped her at the door. He held up both hands in warning, palms out. "You don't want to go in there." He was Bree and Brody's younger cousin, a guy who didn't seem to have a switch to turn off his sense of humor. He was normally flowing with nonstop banter, but he wasn't smiling now.

"I'll be the judge of that." Shiloh tried to push past him, but he reached for her shoulders and held her in place with more strength than she was expecting from a jokester like him. *Great. Another farm boy.* She bit her lower lip. They were accustomed to hard work and had bodies of steel.

"Just wait with me here, alright?" A shock of dark hair fell over his eyes, giving him a devilish look despite his serious expression.

"I've broken guys' hands for less," she snarled.

"Yeah, well, I hope you give me a pass this once." He still didn't budge.

Okay. New tactic. "Who's the ambulance for?" she demanded, fearing the worst. If the victim was in the kitchen, it had to be someone she knew. Star, Bree, or Brody even. *Please, God! Don't let it be Bree.* She was the heart and soul of Anderson Ranch, the woman who cooked, sewed, and served them all every single day.

"It's for Samson Kane." Crew's brows drew together grimly.

"Samson?" Shiloh gasped. She took a step back, feeling utterly blindsided. He was a man she both loved and hated. Someone she'd fought with as much as she'd gotten along with. The love of her sister's life and the father of her unborn niece or nephew. He was also the man she'd been intending to make a few pretty hefty demands of soon — to marry her sister and to tell her everything he'd been keeping secret about the missing pieces of her memories.

And now it might be too late.

She watched, stunned, as his bear-like frame was wheeled from the kitchen, strapped to a gurney. His eyes were closed and his pallor gray. Star Corrigan, Brody's girlfriend, walked beside the gurney, holding his hand. She was an EMT, who was studying to be a nurse. Her heart-shaped face was infused with sadness, telling Shiloh that something was terribly, terribly wrong.

"What happened to him?" Shiloh whispered through numb lips to no one in particular.

She swayed on her feet, and Crew's hand shot out to cup her elbow. "Said his head was hurting real bad while he was pulling security. Then he collapsed."

She drew a sharp breath. "He gets crazy awful headaches sometimes, but he always refuses to do anything about them." And God forbid he darken the door of a hospital to get looked at! He was too suspicious about everybody and everything these days to accept any help.

Crew nodded, looking worried. "Maybe now he'll get the help he needs."

If it's not too late. Remorse slammed into her over

the number of times she'd been furious with Samson since their return from overseas. She'd been furious about the way he ordered everyone around. At his single-minded stubbornness. At his paranoia about everything that moved or breathed. There'd been days she'd seriously wanted to strangle him. And now it might be too late for that, too.

Her feet, which had been rooted to the ground, finally became unstuck. Rushing toward the ambulance, she cried, "I'll go with him."

Star flipped a handful of dark hair over her shoulder, looking like a sad pixie in a flowing white asymmetrical dress that matched Shiloh's. "You can," she said softly. "Or you can hang back and be here for your sister."

"You mean you haven't told her yet?" Now that Shiloh was thinking about it, it was odd that no one else was standing outside by the ambulance with them.

"No." Star's lovely face was set in unbending lines. "I don't want her, Foster, or anyone on Samson's security team to know what's going on until I have him safely checked in at the E.R. To be honest, I would've preferred you didn't find out this soon, either." Though her words were firm, her tone was kind.

"Because you thought we'd try to stop you," Shiloh cried softly. *I wouldn't have, but I can't speak for the others.* She honestly didn't know what Lyon or Foster would've done if they'd been the ones beside Samson when he'd collapsed.

"The thought crossed my mind, yes."

"I'm not here to stand in your way." Shiloh dropped her hand from the bar of Samson's stretcher as the EMTs lifted him aboard the ambulance. "He'll be furious when he wakes up, of course, but you did the right thing. He needs to be at the hospital."

"Thank you." A faint smile tugged at Star's wide, expressive mouth, one that wasn't reflected in her eyes. "I'm going to ride with him, so I can fill out the paperwork necessary to access his VA benefits. I had him sign a few forms before he passed out, so I'm hoping we have everything we need to make this happen."

"So he knew it was bad this time." *Unbelievable.* Mr. Paranoia had finally cooperated with someone trying to help him. Shiloh couldn't have been more grateful to Star for doing everything that she was doing.

"Yes, I think he knew," Star agreed softly.

Shiloh's heart grew heavier. "I don't know what you said or did to gain his trust, but thank you. Thank you with all of my heart."

Star reached over and gently squeezed her hand. "In case you haven't already figured it out for yourself, everyone at Anderson Ranch is family, and family looks after family. Always."

Shiloh nodded damply. "How soon can I tell the others?"

Star looked rueful. "If you can give me about a thirty-minute head start, I'd really appreciate it."

"I can do that." Shiloh was glad the woman didn't expect her to keep the news of Samson's condition from Shayley too long. She couldn't. It wouldn't be right. Well before the concert ended and the patrons were erupting into the parking lot, she would personally ensure that her sister was on her way to the hospital. Gosh, but it was going to be a long night!

Her heart wept as the ambulance doors shut behind Samson and Star. Besides dealing with Samson's collapse, Shiloh would also be saying goodbye to Gabe tonight. He had a red-eye flight to Houston, where he'd be meeting with his agent in the morning. She seemed to remember him saying something about another tour proposal under discussion, something that would last several months and keep him primarily in the Midwest.

I adore you to the moon and back, Gabe. Your music is amazing, and so is the guy who writes it. She was wildly and irrevocably in love with him. What had happened between them in the past month seriously took her breath away. It was still sinking in, actually.

But it was time to let him go. A part of her would always love him, but some creatures were simply too beautiful and majestic to be caged. Gabe was moving on to do wonderful things all over the world, and she wasn't going to stand in his way. She'd been right to keep things light and flirty between them. It was better this way.

The ambulance skidded away from the ranch, lights flashing but sirens curiously silent as they had been upon the EMTs' arrival. Foster, who'd been helping out with the ground crew by directing traffic out front, came jogging around the corner to where Shiloh and Crew were standing.

"What was that all about?" he demanded, jabbing his thumb in the direction of the departing emergency vehicle.

Shiloh stepped up to him and wrapped her arms around his middle. "It was Samson," she informed him quietly. "He collapsed."

"What?" Foster gripped her upper arms. He held her at arm's length, turning pale. "Why didn't you—?" Then his mouth twisted in resigned understanding. "Right. You thought I would stop you from taking him to the hospital." He blew out a frustrated breath. "I probably would have, too, because that's what he would've wanted."

"A day ago, I would've agreed with you, but I'm no longer so sure about that," she sighed, briefly repeating what Star had told her about getting Samson to sign a few forms. Just thinking about the medical bills he was going to run up at the hospital was making her dizzy. She really, really, really hoped Star succeeded in getting him plugged into the many services available for veterans.

With her brain whirling over what she was going to tell Shayley, Shiloh trudged to the front entrance of the B&B. Foster was right on her heels.

Shayley flew through the glass double doors as they approached. "What's going on?" she demanded, glancing pointedly between the two of them. "And don't you dare say nothing. I saw Brody and Bree both running around inside like chickens with their heads cut off." She glared at her sister. "Plus, you guys have been MIA for quite some time now. See?" She slapped her hands down on her hips. "I notice stuff. I'm no longer just a baby sister with her head in the clouds. Someday, you're finally going to get it in your stubborn Marine head that—"

Her words ended on an oomph of surprise as Shiloh stepped forward to enclose her in a bear hug.

"What was that for?" Her voice was muffled against her older sister's shoulder.

"They took Samson to the hospital," Shiloh declared softly. *Sorry, Star. It's not quite the half hour head start you requested, but she deserves to know the truth.*

"You're kidding!" Shayley gave her a small shove to get a better look at her face. "When?"

"Just a few minutes ago." Shiloh hated the way Shayley's face crumpled — not with surprise, but with despair.

"Take me there." Her face was white. Even her lips were colorless. "Now!"

Crew materialized with a set of keys and tossed them to Foster. "Brody said you can take his truck."

Foster caught them in mid-air and immediately stepped to Shayley's side. "Let's go." As tenderly as always, he assisted her across the parking lot as if she was made of spun glass.

"Thanks, Crew." Shiloh dizzily met his dark,

sympathetic gaze, wondering if Star had been right. Maybe these folks at Anderson Ranch really did consider her and her sister to be family now. They sure were acting like it, and she was more grateful than words could express.

He mimed holding a phone to his ear. "Keep us posted, will ya?"

She nodded mutely, too choked to say anything else, and followed after Shayley and Foster. She glanced over her shoulder at him one last time before hopping inside Brody's big white truck. By then, Crew had been converged upon. Lyon, Samson's top security guy, reached him first. He was a beefy ex-Marine with tatted arms and a shaved head. Nash and Zane Wilder, twin brothers who worked on the ranch, skidded up to him next. Before Foster drove them away from the ranch, Shiloh saw Lyon sprint for the parking lot.

As Foster drove them down the two-lane highway toward town, a pair of camouflage painted trucks sped in their direction from behind. Within seconds, they overtook Brody's truck, yanked into the passing lane, and roared by.

"Show offs!" Foster growled, but he made no attempt to increase his speed. "Unlike those bozos, I have precious cargo."

Shiloh stared out the window, grateful that Samson's loyal entourage of ex-soldiers were racing toward the hospital. She could only hope they planned to keep vigil over him, not pull any of their off-the-grid garbage and try to interfere with his medical care.

"Please, God, let him live," she prayed over and over beneath her breath, as they neared their destination.

The sun had nearly finished setting, so the last glow of sunset was fading into blue and purple hues. It was the time of day when few cars remained on the road, farm animals finally settled down, and the world became more peaceful. Usually. Tonight, however, Shiloh knew with sickening certainly that Samson was fighting for his life, and there would be no rest for those who cared for him the most.

A damp sniffle in the otherwise silent cab alerted her to the fact that Shayley, who was sitting in the middle of the long leather seat, was weeping. She was clutching her belly with both hands.

"Are you okay?" Shayley asked quickly. "Is the baby—?"

"No, I'm not okay," her sister sobbed, still clutching her belly. "What if Samson never gets to see the baby?"

Foster reached, white-faced, for one of her hands. "He's gonna pull through, Shay." His voice was low and fierce. "He always does."

Shiloh turned away from his show of protectiveness, though she watched them out of the corner of her eye, envying their intimacy almost as much as she deplored it. The two of them were closer than she thought in-laws should be, but whatever whacked-out relationship they had going on seemed to work for them. One thing she did appreciate about Foster was the way he continued to look out for Shayley. He wasn't simply willing to take a bullet for her sister; he *had* taken a bullet for her already. She had the distinct impression he would do so again without hesitation if the situation called for it.

The phone in the pocket of Shayley's dress vibrated with an incoming call. Still sniffling pitifully, she reached for it.

Shiloh glanced over to scan the caller ID, which was easy to make out on the bright screen inside the dark truck. It was Gabe Romero. Her heart started to pound with a mixture of anticipation and trepidation.

Shayley connected the call without answering it, then handed it to Shiloh. "It's for you," she murmured dismally.

Why did you answer—Lord, love you, girl! Shiloh wasn't in the mood to chat, but she held it to her ear with a sigh. "Hello."

"Shiloh?" Gabe's voice was anxious. "Where are you?"

"We're on our way to the hospital."

"Figured that." His voice was infused with worry. "I just heard what happened to Samson. Any news yet on his condition?"

"No." Her voice sounded shaky, though she had no idea why. Nerves, maybe?

"Would you like me to meet you guys at the hospital?"

Warmth spread through her chest at the thought that he would actually do that for her. "Don't you have a flight to catch?"

"Yep, but I can reschedule it. Just say the word, and I'll head straight there."

She clutched the phone, unsure of what to say next. Yes, she *wanted* him there, but claiming that she *needed* him there wasn't entirely true. She was accustomed to shouldering tough stuff and dealing with it on her own. That's what soldiers were trained to do.

"Listen, Samson has so many friends and family cruising in his direction right now, the hospital won't be able to hold us all. I bet they're already turning folks away at the door," she joked.

"Cute." Gabe sounded both amused and disappointed. "Okay, then. Guess I'll keep that boring appointment in the morning with my agent."

"I hope it goes well," she murmured. *So this is goodbye.* Her heart felt like it was breaking into a million tiny pieces.

"You know what? I don't even care," he retorted with a surprising amount of vehemence. "Right now, my biggest concern is you."

She smiled in the darkness, blinking back tears. "I'm fine. Really." She stopped to clear her throat. "Definitely not the one y'all need to be worried about."

"Too bad, because that's exactly what I'm doing."

She blushed and blinked back more tears. "Safe travels, Gabe."

"I'll be back soon."

Will you? She wasn't holding her breath. Gabe was a rolling stone; they both knew it.

At her silence, he expelled a heavy breath. "I promise, okay?"

Don't, Gabe. Please don't make this any harder than it has to be. "Okay," she whispered and disconnected the line. She'd never been big on long goodbyes.

The next few hours flew past in a blur of white uniforms, intermittent bouts of tears from Shayley, pacing soldiers from Samson's compound, and eventual exhaustion. The doctor walked out of the E.R. a few times to give them updates, but it was pretty much the same stuff.

No change in condition.

Critical but stable.

We're running tests and doing all we can...

Blah blah blah.

It was a bunch of pleasant sounding words intended to soothe, but ended up doing the opposite. Everyone who knew and cared for Samson understood that things weren't looking good for him.

It was around midnight when the second round of bad news hit.

"That's weird!" Shayley was staring with red-rimmed eyes at the cell phone she and Shiloh shared. Though she'd refused Foster's every attempt to return them to the B&B so far, she'd at least agreed to sit in one of the vinyl waiting room chairs. Her feet were propped in a second chair that Foster had scooted up to it.

"What's going on?" Shiloh quickly moved in her direction to peek at the phone screen. What she read there made her freeze.

You are still mine.

You will always be mine.

Horror filled her mouth. *He's back!* Her stalker had finally caught up to her. And he was no longer the nameless, faceless creature she'd feared for so long. He had a name, Arrow Westfield. A demented man who'd purposely set a fire and branded her with it. A man who was supposed to be dead, but wasn't.

"He found me," she declared dully, feeling her stomach turn queasy.

"Who? Gabe?" Her sister squinted at the phone. "It doesn't look like his number."

"No. It's someone else." *We need to delete it, block it, and...hide!* Shiloh shuddered, debating if she should tell her sister what was really going on. *Maybe later.* She already had enough on her plate for one night.

"Who?"

"A secret admirer. Here. Give me that." Without waiting for her sister to hand over the phone, Shiloh snatched it away from her. But before she could delete the message and block the caller, another message came through. This time it was from Bree.

"You and Gabe sounded so wonderful tonight!" Attached to the message was a link that took her to one of Gabe Romero's social media accounts.

A video started to play. It was a recording of the song they'd sung together at the charity concert this evening. Shiloh must not have been standing as far in the shadows as she'd presumed, though, because the videographer had no trouble capturing her face.

Even more disturbing was the number of views the video had received so far — over 10,000! It had gone viral. *Oh, my lands! So that's how Arrow found me.* It didn't explain how he'd gotten ahold of her and her sister's cell phone number. However, there was no denying that the music video was what had led her stalker straight back to her.

Oh, Gabe! What have you done?

CHAPTER 7: HER PROTECTOR

Shiloh

Shiloh frantically searched the hospital waiting room for Foster. Her gaze flitted over worried mothers, whining children, and grim-faced fathers. Apparently, there were a lot of medical emergencies this evening in Hereford.

"What's the matter?" Shayley's high-waisted white dress was wrinkled from too many hours of sitting, and she was starting to look drowsy.

Shoot! I think the better question is what's not the matter, sweetie? "I'm looking for Foster." Shiloh tapped the toe of her boot. She couldn't seem to catch a break. The guy was forever hovering around her and her sister. Now that she actually needed to speak with him, however, he was nowhere to be found. *That figures.*

"I sent him on a coffee run." Shayley gave a gigantic yawn that she didn't bother covering. It was nearly two in the morning, the time of day that most folks were past the point of caring how they looked.

"Pregnant gals can't have caffeine," Shiloh noted mechanically.

"I know, Mom." Shayley stuck out her tongue. "The coffee's for him. He needs to be awake when he drives us back to the B&B."

Yeah, and that needs to happen right now! No more delays. No more waiting for the doctor to reappear with better news. Shiloh fidgeted with her watch, willing Foster to return quickly. She couldn't afford to exit the room to track him down herself, because that would make Shayley vulnerable. There was no way Shiloh was leaving Shayley alone for even a minute now that her stalker was back on the prowl.

The moment Foster's broad shoulders appeared in the entrance to the waiting room, Shiloh made a bee-line in his direction. Or tried to. At the last second, she had to hop out of the way of two boys playing on the floor with Matchbox cars.

"That's some fancy footwork there, Marine." Foster eyed her coolly over the top of his styrofoam coffee mug.

"Where's my coffee?" she demanded irritably.

"Didn't know you wanted any." He took another sip.

"You could've asked." Reaching greedily for his cup, she was relieved when he handed it over without a fight.

"Mmm!" She took a few sips, craving the bracing bite of flavor and snap of caffeine.

Foster watched her, smirking. "Someday you're going to admit you like me."

"Don't press your luck." She took one more sip and reluctantly handed it back. "We need to talk."

"I thought that's what we were doing."

"Just shut up and listen." She stepped closer and lowered her voice. "I am 99.999999% sure we just received a text message from Arrow Westfield."

Foster's jaw tightened, and his large hand shot out to close around her upper arm. "Where's your cell phone?"

"Over there." She nodded at her sister. "Shayley has it."

"I'll dispose of it. We need to get you out of here. Now!" He pivoted her toward the exit and gave her a gentle shove.

"But Shayley—"

"Got it." He lifted his hand to his lips and gave two sharp, ear-piercing whistles that had everyone around them holding their hands to their ears and scowling in their direction.

Lyon and his comrades immediately ceased their pacing and converged on Shiloh and Shayley, using their bodies as shields as they bustled the two women from the waiting room. Instead of returning them to the white pickup they'd borrowed from Brody, the men escorted them straight to the two camouflage painted trucks at the far end of the parking lot.

The back doors were yanked open, and the two sisters were lifted inside the first one.

"Go!" Foster slapped his hand against the side of the vehicle, and the doors were slammed shut.

Shiloh hastily helped buckle Shayley into her seat. To her credit, her younger sister didn't ask questions until they were cruising down the open highway.

"Talk to me," she finally pleaded. Her eyelids were still puffy from earlier, making Shiloh's heart clench with sympathy.

"I..." She had no idea where to begin, no idea how to break the news to her that they had more to worry about than Samson, who still was fighting for his life in the E.R. Unfortunately, they now had more pressing concerns. Neither of them were going to be safe so long as Arrow Westfield was out roaming freely.

"Come on, Shiloh!" her sister pleaded softly. "Quit shutting me out. I've known for a long time that something was wrong." Her face was creased with worry. "Ever since you and Samson got back from overseas, something's been wrong."

Shiloh reached for her hand. "I have a stalker, Shay."

Her sister looked alarmed. "Any particular reason you waited so long to tell me?"

"Because Samson thought that, by taking us off the grid, we'd get rid of him; and we did for a while. But he's back. I'm sorry."

Her sister shook off her hand. "What's there to be

sorry about? Just tell me what we need to do to keep you safe."

Shiloh stared at her in stunned silence. The fact that her sister's only concern was for her safety made her eyes fill with tears. "You've really grown up, kid, haven't you?"

"Duh!" Shayley pointed at her burgeoning belly. "Stuff like this has a way of growing you up real quick."

But Shiloh knew it was more than that. The five-year difference in their ages had mattered a lot more when Shayley was fifteen. But she was twenty-one now and currently bearing the weight of the world on those twenty-one-year-old shoulders.

Shiloh nodded, dashing the back of her hand across her eyes. "His name is Arrow Westfield. We think he's a soldier who got transferred to our unit the day before the big explosion that earned Samson and me our one-way ticket home."

Though her shoulders were sagging with exhaustion, Shayley listened intently. "Have you gone to the police?" The moonlight pouring through the narrow window above their heads illuminated the concern in her blue-gray eyes.

Shiloh gave a huff of disgust. "That's where things get a little complicated. Arrow Westfield is dead." At least on paper he was.

Her sister's eyebrows shot upward. "Um, I know it's late, and we're all tired, but are you really trying to convince me we're dealing with a ghost?"

"Sort of." Shiloh dragged her hands through her hair to pull it away from her face. "We lost a few fellow soldiers during the fire and the explosion it caused. We think Arrow might've switched dog tags with someone else. I know it sounds a little far-fetched, but that's our working theory."

Shayley bit her lower lip in consideration. "If you think that sounds far-fetched, you clearly haven't watched enough movies, girlfriend."

"Maybe not." Shiloh chuckled. There were a lot of normal, every-day things she and her sister hadn't had the luxury of enjoying while growing up. Trips to the movie theater were one of those things.

"So why's this creep after you, anyway?"

"That's the question of the century." Shiloh lowered her hands. "All I know is that when Samson ran into my burning tent, he found Arrow branding me with this." She pointed at the scar on her cheek. *A scar he claims makes me his.* "I was asleep when the fire started, and it doesn't sound like I was all that coherent when Samson found me. Maybe I was drugged. I don't know. Short version of the story is Samson fought off my attacker and carried me through the fire to safety." *Or so Foster claims. I have no memory of it.*

"And you never reported any of this?" Shayley gasped. "Not even to your commander? Why not?"

"Samson tried to, but he was told flat out that the guy was dead." Shiloh traced the scar on her cheek again. "And since we were both treated for

PTSD, I think everyone just sort of wrote off our story to trauma." She shrugged. "We were shipped home with Purple Hearts, glad to be alive and thinking all the bad stuff was behind us, but we were wrong."

"I'm so sorry, Shy." Shayley gripped the edge of her seat as the truck took a sharp turn. "When you accepted Samson's invitation to move off the grid with him and his soldier buddies, I guess I just assumed it was because Dad died leaving us so much debt."

"That was part of it." Shiloh winced as she met her sister's gaze. She'd sorta given up right after the Marines sent her home. Their dad was knocking at death's door, and they had medical bills coming out of their eyeballs since he didn't have insurance. "I was a wreck. Screaming my way through nightmares and hitting the floor every time a car backfired. It wasn't fair to you. So when Samson offered me that security job and told me it came with room and board for both of us, I didn't think twice."

Shayley's eyes were damp by now, too. "But our debts and your health issues weren't the only reasons you accepted the job, huh? You had this creep after you, didn't you?"

Shiloh nodded. "Shortly after I was discharged from the hospital, he started texting me. It didn't stop until Samson moved us onto his compound and got rid of my old cell phone." She stared into the distance at the memory. "At first, we tried to do a little investigating of our own, trying to track Arrow down, but life got in the way."

"You mean me." Shayley grunted and gripped her seat tighter as they bumped their way down a rutty road.

"Hey! Easy there!" Shiloh pounded her hand on the metal wall panel. "Pregnant gal back here, remember?"

The truck slowed down, but didn't stop.

"You were never in my way, sweetie," she assured her sister. "I just meant that we got busy doing other things. I had my security job. Samson was busy dealing with a brother in jail. Then you two fell in love. You know...life. Plus, Arrow stopped texting once we were off the grid. Problem solved, right?"

Shayley's brows rose. "Obviously not. What do you think brought him out of the woodwork after all this time?"

"The charity concert," Shiloh supplied glumly. "Remember how The Texans had a videographer recording their show? Well, they posted it on social media, and it went viral." She grinned, despite the gravity of the situation. "I'm sorta famous right now. Or was." Her smile disappeared. Her stint in the spotlight had been very short-lived. Arrow's reappearance would necessitate taking them right back off the grid. No more budding stardom for her.

"No way!" Shayley slapped her hands down on the vinyl seat for emphasis. "We are not just giving up and crawling away this time. I have a baby on the way, and I have no intention of raising him or her holed up in the backwoods without Internet or central air. I plan to give my child everything you and I missed out on, Shy. T-ball games, birthday parties, pony rides, the whole enchilada."

Her eyes were snapping with determination as the truck rolled to a stop.

Foster yanked open the back door of the tank-like vehicle and held out his arms to Shayley. "Down you go, little mama."

"Where are we?" she demanded, glancing curiously over his shoulder into the darkness.

"Home," he said simply.

Shiloh hopped down unassisted and gazed around them in dismay. They were back in the place she and her sister had always referred to as "tent city." It was a true, off-the-grid community on the rim of a steep canyon. There was a scattering of tents and RVs, campfire sites, piles of chopped wood, and a pair of outhouses. Hammocks and clothes lines were strung between trees, swinging in the night breeze.

Shayley took one look and balked. "Huh-uh! I'm not staying here." She grabbed Foster's arm, forcing him to face her. "I have a baby on the way and a job at the B&B next door that's providing my medical insurance."

"It's only temporary," he soothed, reaching out to tuck a stray lock of hair behind her ear. "I don't like it any more than you do, but it's the one place in the world I know I can keep you safe."

She swung her head out of reach. "Not true. You've been keeping me safe at the B&B for months."

"Yeah, well, things have changed, princess." He dropped his arms. "Shy's stalker is back."

Lyon leaped down from the driver's seat of the second truck and jogged over to them. "The place is secure. We weren't followed. Got a team running patrol on the perimeter."

Though Shiloh was grateful for everything her friends were doing to protect her and her sister, a knot of dread formed in her stomach. She tasted the bitter tang of deja vu. She'd been down this road before, giving up nearly all of her personal freedom to dodge a relentless stalker, and where had it gotten her? Right back to square one, it seemed. It was a discouraging thought. This so wasn't the life she wanted for herself or her sister. Not anymore.

As if reading her thoughts, Shayley fisted her hands on her hips and stared the two men down. "If we go into hiding again, the creep coming after my sister wins. I'm not going to let that happen. Not this time."

Moved by her sister's words, Shiloh stepped forward to slide an arm around her waist. "She's right. I'm done running. Correction. We're done running." The Neeson sisters had always stuck together, and that wasn't going to change now. Shayley was right about needing her job and her medical insurance. The police were already involved; it was time to ramp up security measures and face their problems head on.

Foster lifted his hat to run a hand through his hair. "It's late, and you're both worn to a ribbon. Will you at least stay the night, get some rest, and wait until morning to figure stuff out?"

Shayley lifted her chin. "Under one condition."

"You sound so much like your sister." His lips twitched as he took in her display of stubbornness. "So what's it gonna be?"

"I want your word that you'll take me back to Anderson Ranch in the morning."

"You have it." He inclined his head. "Unless I can't convince you otherwise."

"Which we're going to try our darndest to do," Lyon chimed in. "Unless Brody Anderson has the budget to hire a security team full time at the ranch, we can't spare the guys to guard you 24-7 over there. We gotta get paid to keep food on the table."

He walked away, leaving Shayley to splutter at his statement.

Shiloh hugged her closer. "Listen. Foster's right. We're beat. Let's catch a few Z's. Then we'll come up with a game plan in the morning. One," she assured with a finger raised for emphasis, "that involves returning both of us to the B&B tomorrow."

Shayley sagged against her and seemed to deflate. "Okay, but I'm holding you to the part about returning me to the B&B." She gritted her teeth. "No matter what Lyon says."

Foster waved at the biggest RV on the edge of camp. "Samson's castle is over there, ladies. Make yourself at home." The silver rig gleamed in the moonlight.

Shiloh kept her arm around her sister as they trudged the short distance over the rocky terrain of camp to reach the RV. She reached for the door handle and found it unlocked.

"Well, well, well. Look what the wind blew in," a husky female voice announced from behind them. "If it isn't the diva sisters."

Shiloh slowly pivoted around with her sister to face her favorite ex-soldier on the compound. "Nice to see you, too, Grecia."

Grecia hadn't changed one bit. She was still wearing her fiery red hair short and spiked to the heavens. And, despite it being the middle of the night, she was in full security gear — a dark shirt and matching cargo pants that were knobby with concealed weapons. Shiloh had always suspected the woman slept in her combat boots. Either that, or they'd grown into her skin and were permanently attached.

"So, are you back?" Grecia demanded, pale hands on her slender hips.

"Absolutely not!" Shayley ducked out from beneath her sister's arm to head inside the RV.

Shiloh shrugged. "What can I say? Pregnancy hormones."

"If you say so." Grecia's expression didn't change. She'd never been married or pregnant, nor did she talk much about her past life before moving to the compound. Shiloh wasn't sure if the woman had any family left or not. "It's too bad you're not here to stay. It hasn't been near as exciting around here since you two left."

"What do you mean?" Shiloh cocked her head curiously at her friend.

Grecia shoved her hands in her pockets. "Samson growls around like a wounded bear. I swear the only thing that ever made him seem half-human was Shayley."

Shiloh's heart wrenched. "So have you heard what happened to him?"

She nodded. "Lyon gave me the skinny of it. He's putting us on round-the-clock patrols at the hospital until Sam's well enough to come home."

"Makes sense." Which was why there were no extra security guys to spare right now for other stuff, like guarding the Neeson sisters from a stalker.

"Hey, so..." Grecia looked uncertain. "I know I'm probably crossing a line by mentioning something I'm not supposed to know about but," she met Shiloh's gaze squarely, "for a friend in need, I can work cheap. As in free. So if you need a bodyguard when you return to the B&B, count me in."

"What about—?"

"No buts," Grecia said firmly. "I already cleared it with Lyon. He sorta put himself in charge around here while Samson's out of pocket."

"Okay. I accept your offer, but only if you let me pay you back." Shiloh hadn't been working at the ranch long, so she didn't have much saved up yet. However, she possessed a tiny, rainy day savings.

"I said no buts."

"At least take an IOU."

"Deal. I don't mind you owing me a favor." Grecia held out a fist.

"Deal." Shiloh gave her a fist bump.

"See you in the a.m." Grecia shot a mocking look at the closed curtains of the RV, where a dim light was glowing from the other side. "Or past noon when the beauty queen in there decides to finally roll out of bed."

"Very funny."

"Hey, if the tiara fits…" Grinning, Grecia gave her a two-fingered salute and turned away.

Shiloh hurried inside the RV to find Shayley grumbling.

"Eew! How did we ever live like this?" She was holding up a stained top sheet between two fingers. "I'm so not sleeping on that tonight." She let it drop to the floor and kicked it aside.

"Sheet snob!" Shiloh scoffed good-humoredly.

"Hey, I'm a maid." Shayley straightened her shoulders. "We have high cleanliness standards." She moved to the tiny storage cabinet between the breakfast bar and the rear of the cabin to rummage for fresh linens.

Shiloh eyed the back two bunks and pointed at the one with a bare mattress, figuring it was the least slept in bed and therefore the cleanest. "There." She pointed. "You should take that one."

"Don't mind if I do," her sister sighed as she unearthed a short stack of folded towels. "I hope these have been washed." She gave them a tentative sniff.

Shiloh moved to her side to help lay them across the lower bunk. Then she rolled the last towel to form a makeshift pillow. "It's not the Ritz Carlton, but it'll do for a few hours, sweetie."

Shayley sank onto the bunk with a grateful huff. "What about you?" she asked drowsily.

"I'm not tired yet."

"Liar!" Her sister gave a jaw-cracking yawn.

"Once a Marine, always a Marine, sweetie." Shiloh smiled to note her sister's lashes were already resting against her cheeks. Her breathing soon evened into sleep.

Switching off the recessed lighting, she moved back to the breakfast table to take a seat. Shayley was right; she'd lied about not being tired, but that didn't mean she was ready to go to sleep. She had too much to think about and worry about.

Propping her elbows on the table, she lowered her chin to her hands and allowed her thoughts to drift to happier times. It had been the most incredible feeling in the world to step on stage with Gabe Romero. His kisses had been pretty special, too. The imprint of his lips on hers — warm, tender, and cherishing — would forever be etched in her memories.

As her thoughts drifted, she lost track of time. At one point, she parted the curtains over the table so the moonlight could pour into the dingy cabin. Warmth flooded her insides at the thought that Gabe might right now be staring up at the same moon.

A flash of red and blue lights in the distance jolted her out of the sleepy haze she'd slowly been drifting into. The lights grew closer to the RV, flashing and strobing. It was a police car. She straightened in her seat. What were the police doing here?

Moving to the door of the RV, she pushed it open and stepped outside to watch its approach. All over the clearing, Samson's employees were crawling out of their tents and rising to their feet.

The police car stopped, its doors flew open, and two men stepped out. A voice blared over a microphone. "We're looking for Shiloh Neeson."

She caught her breath. She recognized the voice of Officer Emmitt McCarty from downtown. But what did he want with her?

A new voice spoke over the microphone. "Shiloh, it's me. Gabe Romero. I know you're out there somewhere. Please. We need to talk."

Heart pounding at the promise in his voice, she stepped from the RV into the moonlight. The man standing on the passenger side of the police car jolted at the sight of her. Then he broke into a run.

"Shiloh!" It was Gabe. He reached her and swept her up in his arms, swinging her around and around.

She clung to his neck. "I thought you'd be long

gone by now."

"I was supposed to be, but it didn't feel right to head to the airport after you stopped answering your text messages. I tried tracking you down at the hospital, but they said you left pretty suddenly. Honestly, I was afraid it might not have been completely voluntary, which is the reason for the police escort."

"False alarm. I'm sorry." She stared dizzily at him when he finally quit spinning with her. "I had to ditch my phone. Long story."

"Well, I cancelled my flight, so I have plenty of time to hear it."

"You cancelled it?" she squeaked. As opposed to rescheduling it?

"Yeah. Apparently, Brody proposed to Star tonight, so they'll be getting hitched soon. They asked me to sing at their reception. I wouldn't miss it for the world, so there's no way I can go on that Midwestern tour, after all."

"So what are you saying?" she breathed.

"That I'll be in town for the next few weeks. And I wouldn't mind celebrating that fact over dinner with you tomorrow. Or later today." He shook his head ruefully.

She blinked back the moisture forming in her eyes. "So let me get this straight. You spent all this time and effort tracking me down, just to ask me on a date?"

He gave her a sheepish shrug. "Looks like."

"Then, yes. My answer is yes!" she cried joyfully.

CHAPTER 8: CONFESSIONS

Gabe

Over the next few weeks, Gabe spent every moment he could with Shiloh. As much as he was enjoying getting to know her better, one big black cloud remained hanging over their budding relationship. She flatly refused to talk about her short-lived military career, leaving him to piece it together as best as he could by the small bread crumbs of information that others dropped for him.

"I don't get it," he complained to his brother, two nights before Brody and Star's wedding. "I know she cares for me, but she won't open up and let me in. We date. We kiss, but we don't ever talk things out, as in *really* talk. It's like there's some invisible wall between us."

They were outside, leaning on the white slat fence of the corral where the Anderson Ranch staff gave horseback riding lessons to their B&B guests. It was empty of riders at the moment, though Crew

Anderson was in the ring doing a bit of training with one of the ponies. The sun was beating down, emitting a blistering wave of summer heat.

Gabe didn't mind, since he was already sweaty from his mid-morning run. Plus, he'd spent way too much time inside hunched over his keyboard for the past two years. He'd been trying to make up for it during his stay at Anderson Ranch by spending as much time outdoors as possible. In fact, he was sporting such a dark tan these days that their friends were claiming he and Matt could just about pass for twins.

Matt was wearing a white t-shirt and jeans, with one boot propped on the lowest rung of the fence. His Stetson was pulled low to shade his eyes from the harshest rays of the sun. Rubbing a hand contemplatively over the lower half of his face, he shot his brother an empathetic look. "Shiloh has been through a lot, bro."

"So have I," Gabe sputtered. "But I've given her my life story and gotten next to nothing in return. I'm telling you, she's a closed book, and it's hard to move forward from that."

"You want to move forward, eh?" Matt's voice was both curious and teasing.

"I've fallen for her about as hard as a guy can fall."

"Really? I hadn't noticed. Just thought you had a drooling problem." His brother's eyes twinkled wickedly.

"Haha."

"Seriously, though, she was wounded in the line of duty, and Brody says she's still undergoing therapy for PTSD. Well, to be more accurate, she recently resumed treatment after we got her on our employee insurance plan." Matt watched Crew approach the pony with a saddle, speaking in a low, soothing voice. The pony stood still while he set the saddle blanket on its back, but it snorted and stepped away when he tried to place the saddle on top of the blanket.

Gabe's gaze narrowed on nothing in particular. "Therapy, eh? Is that why Foster Kane and that new chick, Grecia, are always breathing down her neck?"

"Nah." Matt waved a hand. "Foster's just over-doing it as usual, trying to prove he's the perfect brother-in-law. Grecia is her bestie, if I understand the situation correctly — a soldier buddy from way back when. Not really my business, outside of the fact she's been another successful new hire here at Anderson Ranch." He gave a nod of satisfaction. "She's a jack-of-all-trades, picking up the slack wher-ever we need her. If I was running a football team instead of a ranch, I'd seriously consider nominating that feisty little redhead for an M.V.P. award."

Whatever. Gabe wasn't interested in singing Grecia's praises, no matter how hard of a worker she was; he wanted to discuss Shiloh. "I was referring to the way they're always hovering. Seriously, Matt. They never let her out of their sight, which makes it impossible for us to have any alone time."

Matt shrugged. "What about your dates?"

"What about them?"

"Aren't you alone with her then?"

"No," he exploded. "That's what I'm trying to tell you. She refuses to leave the ranch, so our dates are all right here. At the steakhouse, on the back balcony, or on a picnic blanket outside — in plain sight of everyone. We're never alone. Either Foster or Grecia are always somewhere nearby, spying on us."

"Or keeping watch over her," Matt countered slowly.

"How do you figure that?"

Matt shrugged. "It's only a guess, but it sort of adds up, if you think about it."

"I think about it all the time. Trust me," Gabe growled.

"Well, here's what we know. Shiloh and her sister lived completely off the grid for nearly two years after Shiloh returned from overseas. They were sharing a cell phone when I hired them to come work for the B&B; now they no longer own one. Neither sister leaves the ranch except for trips to the hospital to check on Samson or handle prenatal care stuff. And they have friends who never let them out of their sight. My first guess was that one or both of them were hiding from the law, but they passed their background checks with flying colors. It's not likely either of them are trying to outrun a crime spree."

Of course not! That's preposterous! "So what's your theory?"

"The Neeson sisters are worried about something, and they're playing it safe."

Gabe mulled over that piece of information for a moment. "Is that why you've hired a small army to pull security at Brody and Star's wedding?"

Matt snorted. "How did you find out about that?"

Gabe tapped his fist against the fence. "Like they always say, word travels fast in a small town."

"Okay, you caught me. Yes, I've hired plenty of security for the wedding, because my gut says there's something afoot with the Kane and Neeson crowd from next door. I don't know what it is, but I'm not taking any chances. Brody and Star have family and friends flying in from all over the country. It's not worth the risk."

Gabe drummed his fingers on the fence. "Have you asked them if everything's cool? You know, from employer to employee?"

"Other than making it clear I have an open door policy if they ever need anything, no." Matt shook his head. "Sorry, but it's not my place to pry into their personal lives."

"They all seem to be hard workers, too," Gabe mused.

"They work like demons," Matt agreed. "Even Shayley, who's supposed to be taking it easy. A few times, I almost stepped in to say something about curbing her work schedule, but her sister always beats me to it." He smiled. "They really look after each other. Kinda reminds me of a certain pair of brothers back in the day."

"That we did." Gabe swiveled around to lean his shoulders against the fence. "So, I have one more question that's been eating at me."

"Ask away."

"What's your secret, Matt?"

"My secret?" Matt shot a sideways look at him, dark brows raised.

"Everything just seems to be working out for you. Great job. Great wife. Great life."

Matt snorted. "Says the zillionaire celebrity country singer. I think you know a thing or two about success."

"But you're happy," Gabe insisted.

"And you're not?" Matt stopped smiling.

"I don't know." *Not really.* Gabe shrugged. "When I'm in the middle of a concert, there's always this big rush of adrenaline. That's when I feel the most alive. But afterward?" He shook his head. "You can't stay on that big of a high forever. You always come crashing back down, either in the middle of the night or the next day. That's why so many guys in my shoes end up taking performance enhancement stuff. You know, to keep the high going longer."

Matt looked alarmed. "Are you taking anything, bro? Drugs, that is. Legal or illegal?"

"No! Heck no!" Gabe groaned, hating that his brother misunderstood what he was trying to say. "I've had plenty of opportunities, though. That's why

I'm such a loner, I guess. All I do is make a quick showing at the after-action parties. Then I take off."

Matt nodded, looking relieved. "I guess there's something to that saying, after all, about it being lonely at the top."

"Very lonely," Gabe agreed. He crossed his arms and squinted across the gravel drive to the B&B. It was alive with activity, presumably for setting up the wedding that would take place there tomorrow. The front doors were propped open, and ranch hands were busy carrying in boxes and extra chairs. Others were carrying out the round tables that normally graced the large dining area.

"So you want to know the secret to my happiness, eh?" Matt chuckled.

"If there is one." Gabe was no longer so sure that there was. He certainly hadn't run across any secrets yet in his career. Though he was proud of his many accomplishments, a guy couldn't curl up to a fat bank account or a pile of music awards at night. Maybe he was just lonely.

"It's my faith, man."

"Your what?" Gabe shaded his eyes as he glanced over at his brother to make sure he wasn't just messing with him.

"I'm serious." Matt's expression was appropriately sober. "I was a hot mess when I showed up here in Hereford. Mad about my fiancée breaking up with me right after I left the Army for her. Mad about suddenly being homeless and jobless. Just plain mad.

Have I even told you how I ended up here at Anderson Ranch?"

Gabe shook his head. "Nope."

"I got stopped for a speeding ticket."

"Yeah, I think you mentioned that once. But that's all." Gabe was intrigued.

"I was only passing through here to a job interview elsewhere. Or so I thought. But God had other plans for me."

Gabe snickered. "Aw! You trying to say there's a special place in Heaven for speeders?"

Matt's fist shot out and nailed him in the shoulder. "I'm not finished with my story."

"My bad." Gabe liked his own version of the story better. "So was McCarty the officer who busted you?" He was the same officer who'd been on call the night Gabe had requested a police escort to the Kane residence next door.

"Yep." Matt grinned. "He was actually pretty cool about it. Not all in my face and stuff. Don't get me wrong, though. He fully planned to ticket me."

"Sweet guy."

"Just doing his job. Anyway..." Matt shifted from one boot to the other. "While he was writing up my ticket, a big pileup happened on the highway right in front of us. It was bad. We both hurried over there to help out, and the woman I happened to pull from her truck before it exploded was none other than my future wife."

Gabe was amazed. "That's how you met Bree?"

"Eventually. She was sort of out of it at the time. They took her to the hospital, and it didn't seem right to leave town until I was sure she was okay. Met her brother, Brody, in the hospital waiting room. We ended up going to lunch, and he offered me a job when he found out I needed one."

Gabe folded his arms, truly in awe of what he was hearing. "That's an awful lot of coincidences."

"Or a lot of answers to prayer," Matt countered. "Anderson Ranch was really struggling. Brody's a farmer at heart, and Bree just wanted to cook. She's working on a degree in culinary arts."

"And now you're managing the place."

"Yep."

Gabe gave a long, low whistle. "So you were praying for a job, and the Andersons were praying for a ranch manager?" He'd never been a churchgoer, so all this religious talk sounded pretty foreign to him. He respected other people's beliefs, yeah, but he'd never put much stock in stuff like that for himself.

"No, I was pretty much just mad. Saint Brody did all the praying. My praying didn't come until later, actually."

"Oh?"

"Yeah, and it's become my secret sauce, bro."

"Prayer?" Gabe wrinkled his nose, seeing no point in mumbling words to some distant deity who probably had no interest in one lonely country singer.

"More like my entire relationship with God. Prayer is just the way we communicate."

"Seriously, dude? You talk to God?" Again, Gabe scanned his brother's tanned features, wondering if he was joking. He wasn't.

"Every day."

Interesting. "What do you pray for?"

"Everybody I care about. Bree and Brody. The ranch staff. You."

"Thanks." Gabe made a wry face.

"Yeah, I was only acting surprised when you said you weren't happy. I already knew that. Not too long ago, I wasn't happy either, Gabe. You and I didn't exactly have the warmest, cuddliest upbringing in foster care. When you grow up without a family, it leaves a pretty big hole inside you."

A hole. Gabe nodded. That about summed up the way he'd been feeling lately — like there was something missing from his life.

"Like you, I found some comfort for a while in my career. It was exciting being in the military. Got to travel, drive tanks, meet some great people, and shoot big guns. But it was never enough to fill that hole."

"Until Saint Brody got you talking with the Big Guy Upstairs, huh?"

Matt bobbed his head. "Pretty much."

Gabe's head swung impulsively in his younger brother's direction. "Any chance I can get a piece of what you have for myself?" He suddenly, urgently, and intensely wanted to know. "I've tried just about everything else." What could it hurt to give faith a whirl?

"All you have to do is invite Him into your heart, bro."

Gabe's breath came out in a mirthless huff. "I have no idea how to do that."

"Like this." Matt stepped closer and placed his hands on Gabe's shoulders. "Heavenly Father, this is my brother, and he needs you."

The way Matt prayed fascinated Gabe. It was like he was talking to someone who was standing right next to them. As Matt continued praying, a peace like Gabe had never felt before crept over him. It spread into all the empty spaces inside of him — crowding out the angst and loneliness that had been clawing its way through him lately.

When Matt finished praying, he lowered his arms. "So how does it feel to be a friend of God?"

Gabe felt strangely like weeping, but in a good way. "Like I finally got my brother back." All the way. For reals.

"Me, too." Matt leaned in to embrace him again.

They clapped each other on the shoulders and stepped back, eyes glinting suspiciously.

"God has everything under control," Matt assured in a low voice. "You, me, and the situation between you and Shiloh. This is the part where you trust Him to work things out on your behalf."

"Okay." Gabe liked the sound of that. Plus, he was suddenly and ridiculously no longer as concerned about things as he was before his brother had prayed with him. Whistling, he reached into his pocket for the keys to his rental SUV. He tossed them in the air and caught them. "I've got to make a run into town to take care of something. You need anything while I'm out?"

"Nope, but thanks." Matt stuffed his hands in the pockets of his jeans and faced the big red barn. Employees were still bustling in and out of the front doors. "I've gotta get back to setting up for a wedding."

———

Gabe parked in front of the jewelry shop he'd spotted during his last trip into town. It was a sunny, breezy morning. The moment he stepped out of his vehicle, the wind whipped at his t-shirt and jeans and tried to lift his Stetson.

Clapping a hand on top of his hat to hold it down, he strode for the door of the jewelry shop. He had no idea what he was going to purchase for Shiloh, only that he would know the right piece of jewelry when he laid eyes on it.

She was a maid, so she obviously wasn't rolling in cash. The only adornments he'd ever seen her wear were her sports watch and dog tags. For that reason, he wanted to buy her something nice. Something that would make her feel special. Nothing too over the top, though, because she wasn't that kind of girl.

"Gabe Romero?"

The shock in the man's voice jolted Gabe from his

pleasant train of thought. He paused with his hand on the doorknob to the jewelry shop and glanced around to locate the owner of the voice.

"Who's asking?" The only person standing anywhere near him was a construction worker in a yellow hard hat and overalls. Tinted goggles covered his eyes, and a dusty kerchief was tied over the lower half of his face. He was holding what looked to be a blowtorch, a blue canister with a slender silver nozzle.

"I am." The construction worker compressed the trigger, and flames blasted from the nozzle of his torch.

"Whoa!" Gabe lunged back a step as the guy advanced on him.

"She belongs to me, Mr. Country Singer, not you. She will always be mine, so you'd best back off." The guy waved the torch this way and that like a sword, sending flames close enough to Gabe to singe the hair on his arms.

"What are you talking about?" There was little time to think, so Gabe simply acted. Fortunately, he had a few self-defense classes under his belt. He kicked the next time the maniac swung the blow-torch in his direction, hoping to knock the canister from his gloved hands.

His attacker leaped back to avoid the kick and, instead, trained the torch directly on Gabe's boot. The rubber sole of it hissed and bubbled beneath the sudden blast of fire.

Then, without warning, the guy took off sprinting down a side alley. Gabe tried to follow him, but the gummy, sticky bottom of his boot slowed him down. By the time he returned to the front of the jewelry store, a small cluster of townsfolk had gathered.

"Are you okay, sir?" a man yelled to him. He was a silvery-haired fellow in a rubber apron with a pair of jeweler's glasses pushed high on his forehead.

"We saw it all," a middle-aged woman declared breathlessly, clinging to the arm of a man Gabe could only assume was her husband. "We were inside picking out the perfect ring for—"

"That doesn't matter, honey," the man at her side interrupted, patting her hand. "We called the police, son. They said they'll be here in two snaps."

Sure enough, sirens were already blaring in the distance.

Officer Emmitt McCarty rolled up to the curb and lowered his window. "You again, huh?" He waggled his dark brows at Gabe as he set his emergency brake and stepped out of his cruiser. Strolling around the car, he drawled, "I guess your visit to the Kane compound wasn't exciting enough." He was a cowboy cop, from his Stetson to his boots. A navy uniform shirt boasting a silver badge was tucked into a pair of jeans.

Gabe lifted his singed boot. "Believe me, I have better ideas about how to have fun."

"You and me both, Romero." Emmitt squatted down for a closer inspection. "So this is what a blowtorch does to a man's boot. Hmm." He shook his head. "You see something new every day in my line of work." He took out his cell phone and snapped a few pics. "Mind telling me what happened?"

Gabe quickly related how the construction worker had seemingly appeared out of nowhere, yelling and waving his blowtorch. "He said 'she' belonged to him and for me to back off, but he never said who 'she' was."

"Any ideas?" Emmitt eyed him sharply.

"Yeah, but I'd rather share them in private, if you don't mind."

"I don't mind. Did you get a good look at him?"

Gabe had to ponder the question a moment. Though he'd faced the guy head-on, he'd never really gotten a good look at him, come to think of it. "Medium build, I guess. Few inches shorter than me. Blue overalls, gloves, yellow hard hat, tinted goggles, and a navy kerchief tied over the lower half of his face."

"Not much to go on, unless anyone snagged a pic." Emmitt glanced around their small group. "Did any of you take a picture of the guy?"

"I'm sorry," the middle-aged woman quavered. "It all happened so fast!"

"Was he showing any skin?" Emmitt pressed, returning his gaze to Gabe's.

"Yeah. He was white, I think. Or pinkish-white." He frowned. "I'm not sure. Maybe his face was flushed or something."

"We'll put an APB out for this joker." Emmitt shook his head. "But unless he's crazy enough to continue waving his blowtorch around town, we really don't have much to go on."

I disagree. For the first time in weeks, Gabe felt like he had plenty to go on. Although some maniac had just tried to light him on fire, he felt strangely elated. His attacker had to be the reason everyone at the ranch was being so protective of Shiloh. He didn't know who he was dealing with yet, whether an ex-boyfriend, ex-husband, or some other creep. However, he fully intended to find out.

In the end, Officer Emmitt McCarty opted to follow Gabe back to the ranch. They parked in the B&B customer lot and stepped out to confer one last time before heading inside.

"I'd like to speak to her first, if that's okay." Gabe frowned as he scanned the faces of the ranch hands coming and going from the front entrance. Shiloh was not among them.

"That's not how this usually works, Romero." Emmitt looked conflicted as he pulled out a pen and pad. "It's best to get my reports hot off the grill, so to speak — not after folks have time to compare and coordinate their stories."

Gabe stared, aghast. "She wasn't even there when it happened. It's just that...I care for her, alright? I'm only asking for a couple of minutes."

"Gabe?"

The sound of Shiloh's voice had him spinning around on the asphalt.

She was jogging down the steps of the sunroom to the main ranch house, where Brody and Matt's business office was located. "Is everything okay?"

"Yeah." Glancing back at Officer McCarty and silently begging him to stay put, Gabe hurried in her direction. He couldn't help drinking in her slender, athletic form beneath her faded shirt and jeans. She was wearing no makeup as usual, and her long, blonde hair was swinging sassily from a ponytail that his fingers itched to tweak. She was seriously one of those rare, gorgeous creatures who would probably look great in a paper sack.

She wrinkled her nose as he drew closer. "What's that smell?" Her lovely oval features grew taut, as if not liking the scent. "If I had to guess, I'd say it's burning rubber."

He grimaced at her and held up his burned boot. "Bingo. You've got the schnozzle of a bloodhound."

"What happened? Did you step inside a volcano?" she teased.

"No. I was shopping in downtown Hereford, and a guy came after me with a blowtorch." He watched closely for her reaction.

She paled a few degrees. "Please tell me you're kidding."

"I wish I was. He said 'she belongs to me' and warned me to back off, though he never identified who 'she' was. I have my suspicions, of course."

"Omigosh, Gabe!" She swayed on her feet. "I never meant to put you in danger like this."

"I'm okay, darling."

"No, you're not!" Her voice rose to a frantic pitch. "Nothing is okay right now. Samson is fighting for his life in the hospital, Shayley is about to pop out a baby, and you've somehow landed yourself in the crosshairs of the very maniac who's been turning my world into a living hell." Her voice broke.

Gabe drew her into his arms. "Hey! We're going to get through this, okay?"

She writhed in his grasp, pulling back to gaze anxiously up at him. "If you had any sense, you'd get on that plane and fly as far from here as you can." Her eyes were red-rimmed, and she was close to weeping.

"I'm not going anywhere, darling." He flicked a finger down her undamaged cheek. "I'm right where I want to be."

As the first tear broke loose and skidded down her face, Officer McCarty lightly cleared his throat from behind them.

"I hate to interrupt, but I have a few questions to ask you, Miss Neeson."

CHAPTER 9: WEDDING BELLS & ROSE PETALS

Shiloh

The day of Brody and Star's wedding dawned bright and beautiful. It was warm but not too hot — mostly clear, with only a hint of clouds. Shiloh rolled out of bed, feeling tired and out of sorts. She also wasn't all that thrilled about having to don the ruffly white cotton dress she'd worn to the last concert. *Pardon me, folks, but I'm just not a dress-up kinda gal.*

Part of her crabbiness was probably coming from the fact that she hadn't slept much since Officer Emmitt McCarty's trip to Anderson Ranch. Dread had robbed her of her appetite and peace of mind. There was a sense of foreboding in her gut that she simply couldn't shake. She was relieved not to have to continue keeping her ugly secret from Gabe, though he probably thought she was out of her mind to be claiming a dead man was stalking her. It was way too bad the only person who could confirm her story was lying in a coma.

With a sigh of sheer frustration, she dragged her limbs to the shower and turned the water to scalding.

"Make it quick in there!" Shayley called through the door. "Pregnant ladies' bladders don't last long."

Shiloh chuckled, despite her grumpy mood. Her sister was forever making jokes about her condition, though she was probably feeling miserable most of the time. Shiloh couldn't fathom what it must feel like to have a little human growing inside her body. She hoped with all of her might that Shayley wasn't just trying to make the best of a bad situation; she hoped that her sister was actually ready and wanting to be a mother. Because that's exactly what was going to happen soon.

She allowed the hot water to work its magic on her and finish waking her up, which it did. Stepping out of the shower, she toweled off in billows of steam.

"And don't forget to turn on the exhaust fan!" Shayley called. "I don't want to step into a sauna. Ugh!"

Oops! Shiloh hastily flipped on the switch to the exhaust fan.

"I heard that!"

Shiloh grinned as she shimmed into her dress and turned to face the mirror over the vanity to see how she looked. It was completely steamed over from her shower. *Guess I'll be putting on my makeup and styling my hair somewhere else.*

As she pulled open the bathroom door, she nearly

ran into her sister. "Sorry about the sauna," she muttered, breezing guiltily past.

Her younger sister peered inside the bathroom and moaned. "OMG! Did you get any water at all on you, Shy? Because I'm pretty sure most of it's in the floor."

"I'll clean it up." Shiloh hurried back to the bathroom to see what her sister was talking about. "Sorry. I know I'm a slob."

"Nope. Nope. Nope." Shayley shut the door in her face. "My turn in the bathroom, girlfriend."

"Well, I don't want you falling on the wet tile," Shiloh protested through the door.

"Don't worry. I'm standing on your towel," her sister returned cheerfully. "Guess you'll have to swap it out for a new one."

Shiloh snorted out a laugh and turned away. Yeah, her sister's sense of humor was very much still intact. She was going to be alright. Shiloh wished she could say the same for Samson Kane.

His condition hadn't changed much during the past month. According to the doctors, every cell is his body was flat worn out. The machines he was hooked up to were still registering brain activity, but his organs and limbs were just too weak for him to stand up and resume his normal activities. The only good news they could give was that he was no longer in a constant coma. Rather, he was drifting in and out of consciousness. Lately, when they visited him, they could feel his fingers move. Shayley even claimed he'd whispered something to her once, though she'd not been able to understand what he said.

"Please get well, Samson," Shiloh whispered beneath her breath. Heaven knew they had their differences, but he'd done his best to look after her and her sister. Not to mention her sister was in love with him and carrying his child. *We need you to come back to us. Please!*

It was with a heavy heart that she moved to the mirrored closet door to style her hair. Weary blue-gray eyes stared back at her from a too-thin, oval face. So much for her scalding shower! *I still look tired.* She was half-tempted to change into a plaid shirt and pair of jeans and try to fade into the ranks of those who'd been hired to pull security.

However, her sister would probably pitch a fit. Lately, she'd been harping about how she wanted some semblance of normalcy back in their lives before her child was born. She was well on her way to making friends with all the amazing owners of Anderson Ranch and their staff members. She seemed to have bought into that whole we're-all-family-now thing that the Andersons and Romeros tried to cultivate among their employees.

They weren't family, of course. None of them were, no matter how many staff dinners they served and how much hospitality they oozed. At the end of the day, Shiloh and Shayley Neeson were still, and always would be, nothing more than maids. The hired help. The have-nots. But Shiloh had to hand it to the Andersons and Romeros; they meant well. They genuinely tried to foster a sense of family and community at the B&B.

After piddling in front of the mirror a while longer, wondering what Gabe had ever seen in such a skinny, washed-out ex-Marine, Shiloh ended up leaving her hair down. The first time Gabe had looked at her, as in *really, really* looked, she had her hair down. She waited until Shayley returned to the room to beg for her assistance in applying makeup.

"What would you do without me here to dress you and make you beautiful?" Shayley scolded as she obligingly rubbed on foundation and powdered her sister's cheeks and nose.

That was an easy answer in Shiloh's book. "I hope I never have to find out, sweetie."

"You won't. Promise!" Shayley gave her nose an extra powdery tap for emphasis.

Then the sisters glided to the elevator in a cloud of body mist and hairspray fumes. The ride to the main gathering area in the B&B was short. They stepped into the crowd of milling guests and glanced around.

There were a ton of faces they didn't recognize, so they lingered on the side of the room, absorbing the number of changes that had taken place at the B&B during the last couple of days. The ceiling was literally drenched with tiny white lights — thousands of them. It brought to mind a star-studded sky, which was wildly appropriate considering that the bride's name was Star.

Instead of the linen-draped round tables that normally filled the room, rows of honey-gold oak chairs were resting in neat rows. The seat backs were tied with gauzy white bows, whose ends hung gracefully down. The chairs were spaced in such a way that they formed ten neat rows on each side of the room, with a wide center aisle between them. Presumably, it was for the bride's forthcoming promenade to the white rose trellis resting in front of the stage.

Though Shiloh scanned the room for him, there was no sign of Gabe Romero.

"Looking for someone?" her sister teased, gently elbowing her in the ribs.

"Don't know what you're talking about," Shiloh returned irritably.

"Oh, I think you do." Her sister batted her lashes in a way that Shiloh found to be one hundred percent obnoxious.

Foster materialized in front of them, gazing down at Shayley as if she was the only woman in the room. Or at least the only one who mattered.

He'd aged, in Shiloh's opinion, since his brother had been taken to the hospital. His dark brown hair had grown shaggier on top, and he now sported a short beard. Weary resignation tightened the corners of his mouth and cast shadows beneath his eyes. It was plain he was worried about Samson, which he had every right to be. What gave Shiloh mixed feelings was the way the tension in his broad shoulders always seemed to relax at the sight of Shayley. He seriously lit up around her. Every. Single. Time.

His gaze fell to her pouting lips.

"Tell me how nice I look, Foster," she demanded, placing her slender hands on her hips. "All Shiloh has done is snap and growl ever since she woke up this morning." She wrinkled her nose at her sister. "And steam up the bathroom and leave water all over the floor and—"

"I get it!" Shiloh raised both hands. "I'm a horrible person. Excuse me for living."

"See what I mean?" Shayley waved at her in mock disgust.

Foster looked mildly abashed. "I'm a guy, which means you ladies should probably leave me out of stuff like this."

Shayley made a face at him. "Fine. But you're not getting out of lying to me about how beautiful I am. When I looked in the mirror this morning and saw a beached whale staring back..." She made a moaning sound and covered her face with her hands.

Chuckling, Foster gently pried her fingers away from her eyes. "Come on. Let me at least have a look at you before I issue a verdict."

She dropped her hands from her face without letting go of his. "And the jury says?"

Using their joined hands, he tugged her closer to press a kiss to her forehead. "You are the most beautiful woman I've ever known, Shay. On the inside, the outside, and everywhere in between. My brother would have been lost without you for the last couple of years. And so would I."

When he took a step back, her eyes were shining with dampness and gratitude. "That was seriously the nicest thing anyone has ever said about me." Then her lips twitched. "You are a very good liar."

His dark brows shot upward. "I wasn't—"

Ignoring his protest, she spun back to face her sister, dropping his hands. "Now say something nice about my sister."

"Ah-h-h-h..." He laughed, clearly pretending that nothing came to mind.

"Not such a good liar, after all, are we?" Shiloh's sugary sweet tone was laced with venom.

His dark eyes twinkled. "I'm just trying to figure out if you're going to hurt me the most if I say something nice or keep my mouth shut."

"Down, boy." She curled her upper lip at him. "Your torture session was a onetime thing."

"Torture!" Shayley gasped, looking more fascinated than alarmed. Her head swung between the two of them. "When was it, and how did I miss it?"

The band behind the stage curtains struck the opening notes of a familiar country song called *One Little Promise*. It was one of Shiloh's favorite songs by The Texans, a song she now understood had probably been written by Gabe Romero, himself.

"Saved by the bell," Foster muttered in exaggerated relief. "Come on, ladies. Let's grab some seats before they fill up." He gently eased himself between the sisters and propelled them forward with a hand on each of their shoulders.

"Luckiest guy in the house," he muttered in Shiloh's ear. "I get to escort two hot chicks to their seats instead of one." He made a big show of seating himself between them, stretching his arms across the backs of their seats. Then he crossed one leg over the other like an uber-satisfied mafia don.

Shiloh immediately stood. "Move over." She pointed at the seat she'd just vacated. "Now. Or I seriously will hurt you."

"You can't," he mocked. "You said the torture session was a onetime thing."

"I'll make an exception," she threatened.

"There are witnesses," he pointed, waggling a finger in the air at her. "Lots of them."

"I'm sure Officer McCarty will be happy to arrest me." She swatted at his shoulder, trying not to laugh.

With one last searching look at her, he moved over. "I'm not as bad as you think," he muttered for her ears alone as he settled into the seat on the other side of her.

"You have no idea what I think," she retorted, smoothing her skirt over her knees.

"I'd like to." Again, he kept his voice low. "Like I said before, we're stuck with each other. You might as well quit fighting it."

She expelled a silent huff. "I know."

He seemed satisfied by her answer. The opening

notes of the Wedding March sounded, eliminating the need for her to say more.

As Star Corrigan sashayed down the aisle on the arm of her beaming father, Shiloh felt the burn of tears. The bride's curvy frame was encased in a mermaid-cut dress of white lace that flattered the hourglass flair of her hips. She was, by far, not the skinniest bride in the world, but Shiloh would've bet all the money she didn't possess that Star was the happiest one.

Glancing out of the corner of her eye, she noted the tremble to her sister's lips and the wistfulness in her stance. It made Shiloh want to march straight to the hospital and shake the snot out of Samson. This was what he should have given her sister — a wedding day with all the frills. It didn't matter if the pomp and circumstances of the ceremony itself meant nothing to him; it would mean everything to her sister.

She impulsively leaned closer to Foster and hissed in his ear, "Shayley is going to get her turn walking down the aisle, so help me God!"

His bored expression sharpened, and he treated her to a strange look. Then he slowly nodded his agreement.

Satisfied that he would side with her when it came time to have that conversation with his brother, she settled back in her seat. However, she felt Foster's eyes on her several times through the remainder of the short ceremony.

"What?" she snapped in a low voice as they stood for Star and Brody's promenade back up the aisle.

He waited to respond until the bride and groom positioned themselves at the beginning of the receiving line where the rest of the wedding party was assembled. The guests slowly emptied from their seats to form a line. "You're an amazing woman, Shiloh Neeson. A bit on the hard-hearted side, but nothing I can't live with." His smirk was back.

"Aw!" Shayley reached for his arm as they exited their row, presumably to steady herself. "Did you finally say something nice to my sister?"

———

Shiloh knew Brody better than she knew Star, but she didn't dare skip the receiving line. The woman was married to one of her bosses now, which made her a boss by association. *I think.* Star worked in the medical field, and Shiloh wasn't sure if that would change now that she was married.

She, her sister, and Foster ended up near the end of the long line of guests. While they waited to greet the happy newlyweds, the stage curtains opened. Gabe and his band crooned their way through the first song he'd planned for the reception.

Matt and Bree had opted to cater the food, so the entire staff at Anderson Ranch could be off duty for the event. Well, mostly off duty. Several of them were either on call or light duty to serve the needs of the B&B guests who were still in residence.

Shiloh reached the happy bride and groom in the receiving line just in time to hear someone calling for Star to throw her flowers.

"Omigosh!" Star gasped, throwing a laughing look at her new husband. "I almost forgot."

He blew her a kiss. "It's not too late."

Her bridesmaids were already clustering around — her two younger sisters plus Bree Romero. Star happened to glance up and catch Shiloh's eye, to her intense dismay.

She waved a hand gaily, beckoning Shiloh and Shayley forward. "Get over here!"

With an inward sigh of resignation, Shiloh touched her sister's wrist. "I think we're being paged."

"Sweet!" Shayley didn't hesitate to join the happy cluster of bridesmaids.

Shiloh followed at a more reluctant pace. She tried to hang back a bit, but Star waved her closer. "You're part of the family now."

Right. Everyone keeps saying that. Shiloh forced a smile, wanting to believe her. Wanting, more than anything, to be a part of the undercurrent of joy that was coursing through the room.

She watched as Star waved her bouquet of white roses, sunflowers, and baby's breath. The bridesmaids stepped back to give her more room, forming a loose circle around her. A few other young women from the audience squealed and rushed forward to join them.

"Close your eyes!" Bree ordered.

Star squeezed her eyes shut, sweeping her long dark lashes against her flushed cheeks.

"Now toss 'em like you mean it!" Bree sang out.

Star bent at her knees for leverage, then sent the bouquet sailing. The blooms and trailing ribbons seemed to rise in slow motion. Then they made a graceful arc and started to descend, gathering speed as they plummeted back down to the hopeful crowd of females below.

To Shiloh's surprise, the flowers seemed to be heading directly for her. She had two choices — to duck out of the way or make the catch. At the last second, her hand shot out as if it had a mind of its own, and she found herself staring down at the gorgeous bouquet.

Oh, my lands! Now what?

There was clapping, cheering, and more female squealing as the bridesmaids pressed closer to shower Shiloh with romantic well wishes.

Why did I catch them? The bouquet might as well have been a snake ready to strike as far as Shiloh was concerned.

"Oo, Shy!" Shayley gave her a coy smile. "Got something to tell me?"

Shiloh treated her to a hard, warning look. *Don't you dare look at the stage! Don't do it! Don't do it!*

But of course her sister did.

Gabe Romero, who must have left the stage at some point — possibly to greet the bride and groom — leaped back onto the stage and reached for the microphone. "Congratulations Star and Brody Anderson! This song is for you." He signaled for his band to transition the music to the next number.

Shiloh felt his eyes on her as he started to sing. Unable to resist, she lifted her head to meet his gaze and found him singing directly to her.

It was *Under the Texas Stars,* the same song they'd sung together at the charity concert. Without dropping her gaze, he moved to sit on the edge of the stage. His boots dangling over the edge were as shiny as black glass. As he sang the second line, he produced a second microphone and held it out to her.

Me? She pressed a hand to her chest. *You want me to sing with you again?*

Following his gaze, several of the wedding guests started to clap and cheer encouragement her way. Clearly, they remembered the last time she'd sung with him.

What to do? What to do? After a moment, she moved in his direction. There was no more point in worrying about her anonymity. Her stalker already knew where she was. It was only a matter of time before he made his next move, which likely wouldn't be today considering how many security guys were weaving their way through the crowd.

However, she was mindful of the fact that Arrow

Westfield had essentially issued a death threat to the man she cared about. The sooner she made her getaway from the crowd of wedding guests and their flashing cameras, the better.

She glided in Gabe's direction. But instead of taking the microphone he was holding out to her, she bent her head closer to it. Call it hopeless vanity, but she allowed her long, blonde hair to swing forward and form a curtain between them to hide her scarred cheek.

"So many stars that I lose myself in them," she sang breathily into the mike. Then she made the mistake of glancing up at him.

There was so much adoration and longing in his dark gaze that it took her breath away, making it impossible for her to keep singing. Feeling dizzy with too many sensations to name, she spun away from the stage, leaving him to finish the song alone.

Yes, it was cowardly of her — possibly the most un-Marine like thing she'd ever done in her life — but she basically ran from the room.

CHAPTER 10: LAST STAND

Shiloh

Shiloh didn't immediately return to her room at the B&B. Her nerves were too jangled from her latest encounter with Gabe, so she took a stroll around the horse corral, instead. She sensed the two of them were due for a showdown. He'd made his feelings about her pretty clear on a number of dates lately, but she wasn't one hundred percent sure what she planned to do about it.

She'd long since stopped telling herself that her hesitation to move forward in their relationship had anything to do with her stalker. It was more than that – so much more than that, stemming all the way to her childhood.

Her mother had died when she was such a young girl that she barely remembered her. And because her father had to be gone so much with his job, it had pretty much been up to her to raise her baby sister.

Shiloh had been forced to grow up too soon, to rely on herself and no one else for so long that she'd honestly forgotten how to.

Or didn't want to.

Or was afraid to.

The moment she let Gabe in, she knew she would be vulnerable in ways she'd never allowed herself to be vulnerable before. Swinging the wedding bouquet against her side as she walked, she gazed off into the distance.

She would also be loved if she decided to pursue a relationship with Gabe. And she would no longer be alone. As far as her ties to Shayley were concerned, the kid had finally grown up. She already had a life of her own and soon wouldn't be needing Shiloh as much as she used to, or at least not in the same way. Her younger sister had blossomed like grass right through the tough sidewalk that paved their lives. No matter what happened to Samson, Shayley was going to be alright. Foster would see that she was.

Which left Shiloh with one last decision — what to do about Gabe Romero? Was it finally her turn to make a grab at happiness?

"Ma'am?"

Shiloh glanced up as an older gentleman approached her. He was wearing a powder blue polyester suit, a throwback to days gone by, and walking with a slow, hitching motion while leaning on his cane.

"Yes, sir. May I help you?" She immediately snapped back into the role of a B&B employee, ready to answer questions and serve customers.

"I sure hope so." His face was lined like an ancient piece of parchment, and he had that old man tremor to his voice. "Are you Shiloh Neeson?"

Though she kept her best customer service smile pasted on, she stiffened. "How did you know my name?"

"I didn't, but it's written here on this..." His words dwindled as he reached inside his blazer, making her fingers long to be holding a revolver. He unearthed a single white envelope and handed it over.

"A gentleman stopped me at the gate on the way here and begged me to deliver this to you. Normally I wouldn't involve myself in other folks' business like that, but he seemed desperate. He even offered to pay me, though I refused."

"Thank you." Shiloh accepted the envelope with cold fingers. "Is there anything else I can do for you, sir?"

"No, but thank you." He tipped back his head and closed his eyes, allowing the canyon breeze to riffle through his thinning hair. "Now that I've done my good deed for the day, I'm going to enjoy this farm-fresh air for a bit." He cracked his eyelids open to give her a wobbly smile. "At least until the Mrs. comes looking for me and scolds me into returning to the party."

"And you are?" she prodded.

"Jack Corrigan, the bride's great-uncle."

"Nice to meet you, Mr. Corrigan," she returned mechanically, not bothering to enlighten him to the fact that he'd just assisted a serial killer in getting a message to her.

He nodded kindly at her.

She hurried around the back side of the B&B to the employee entrance, ripping open the envelope as she walked. A plain sheet of white computer paper was inside. A short, cryptic message was written on it.

Samson is finally awake and ready to pay for his sins.

Shiloh caught her breath, instantly knowing who the message was from. But what did it mean? The best she could figure was that Arrow Westfield was planning some sort of revenge against the man who'd stopped him during his first assault attempt.

Over my dead body are you going to attack a war hero in a coma, you coward! Samson had risked his life to protect hers once before; it was her turn to protect him. Dashing through the kitchen, she made her way to Bree's small private office and picked up the phone. Dialing the hospital, she hastily identified herself.

"Yes, ah...I need to know the status of Samson Kane. Is he awake yet?"

The receptionist transferred her to the nurse's station of the inpatient ward on the second floor. Shiloh breathlessly repeated her question.

"No, love," the nurse answered gently. "His condition is the same as yesterday. He's been moving his fingers and toes a little more, though, and there's been more eye movement today so we're hopeful he's going to wake up soon."

"Okay. Thank you." Shiloh set down the phone in its cradle. Her worst fears were confirmed. Samson was close to waking up, and somehow Arrow Westfield was aware of that fact.

Which meant he was nearby.

Possibly at the hospital right now.

And he was waiting for her.

Bring. It. On. She couldn't remember the last time she'd felt this angry. This righteously indignant. *You want to tango, Arrow Westfield? Okay. Let's dance.* She wasn't meeting him unarmed, though.

Creeping her way softly up the back stairwell, she made her way to the room she shared with Shayley. With shaking fingers, she punched in the combination to their small safe in the closet. Then she withdrew her pistol. Thankfully, Texas was an open carry state, and she was licensed to carry. Tucking it into the side of her boot, she made her way back down the stairs.

One angry Marine is coming your way, you maniac! Returning to Bree's office, she borrowed the keys to her new red truck. *I'm so sorry, Bree! You can fire me later.* Only one thing mattered now, and that was ending the nightmare she and Samson had been living in for so long.

Bree's truck was parked along the back side of the

B&B. As Shiloh made her way to it, she heard a man shout her name. Not wanting anyone to slow her progress, however, she pretended she didn't hear. It was probably just Foster.

Keeping her head bent over the steering wheel, she turned the key in the ignition and started rolling forward. She inched her way around the big red barn at a snail's pace, mindful of the fact that there were guests milling around the property. On the main driveway leading away from the main ranch house, she let her foot off the brake and coasted faster. The moment she reached the highway, she mashed the gas pedal.

It was only a fifteen to twenty-minute drive downtown to the hospital. Though Shiloh was sorely tempted to speed, she resisted, not wanting to get stopped for a speeding ticket. Instead of parking in the main parking garage, she circled the hospital to ensure she wasn't being followed and selected a spot near the E.R.

No sooner had she stepped into the main hallway leading to the elevators did the fire alarms start to wail. Emergency lights flickered along the walls. All around her, she could hear walkie talkies going off and voices shouting, "Code red! Code red!"

A man's voice blared across the intercom system. "May I have your attention, please? May I have your attention, please? Please make your way in an orderly fashion to the nearest exit. We are evacuating the hospital due to a fire. I repeat. Please make your way to the nearest..."

Ha! Really, Arrow? A fire? How original...not! She was clearly dealing with some sort of pyromaniac.

She watched for several minutes as medical personnel and patients erupted non-stop from the elevators. Nurses and medics pushed patients in hospital beds. Other uniformed employees guided patients outside who were hanging on to rolling I.V.s.

Shiloh waited until the flood of people moving off the elevators slowed to a trickle, indicating that the second floor was nearly empty. Then, pushing her way against the crowd, she made her way to the stairwell.

"Ma'am! This way, please, ma'am!" a nurse called, anxiously waving both arms at her.

Pretending not to see her, Shiloh pushed open the big metal door leading to the stairwell and dashed up the stairs.

An inferno of heat and smoke met her the moment she stepped into the second story hallway. Sprinklers were spraying in all directions. Blinking and coughing, she tore the sheet off an empty gurney resting against the wall and held it over her mouth and nose. Then she spun in a full circle.

"Where are you, Arrow Westfield?" she screamed.

The fire alarms were so loud and her voice was so muffled beneath the white fabric that she doubted anyone could hear her. On an angry whim, she reached up to tear off a section of the sheet and tied it behind her head. Once her arms were free, she grabbed the handles of an abandoned wheelchair and began ramming it into the side of the gurney. With a little luck, the loud clanging noise would announce her presence.

The figure of a man stepped jerkily through the clouds of smoke and made his way toward her. He was a complete stranger to her. She didn't recognize his stocky build, nor the mottled features of the man staring at her through the eye shield of a gas mask. She did, however, recognize the blue canister he was holding and the orange lava flames that were shooting from it.

He met the description of the same man with the blowtorch who had attacked Gabe the other day.

"What do you want from me?" she screamed, backing up a few steps. *Why did you choose me?*

It took a moment for her dazed brain to register the fact that the reason the man was moving so slowly toward her was because he was on fire. Flames were licking their way up his pants legs, and no wonder. The blowtorch he was so carelessly waving around was lighting his own clothing. To her horror, he kept walking toward her, however. His steps were dogged, and the hard light in his eyes settled on her with unerring determination.

So you want to die and take me with you, huh? She bent to reach for the pistol in her boot and came up with it, aiming with both hands. But before she could pull the trigger, a second man emerged from the smoke.

It was Samson. A goose egg was forming on his forehead, and a trickle of blood ran from it. He'd been hit!

His dark, glassy eyes briefly met hers. For a moment, they were soldiers again on the battlefield, united against a common enemy. He silently telegraphed his intentions. Then he lunged forward and fell on her would-be attacker, using the weight of his enormous frame to bring the man down. The two men went crashing to the floor. The blue canister bounced to one side, and the flames coming from the nozzle extinguished.

Neither man moved, and the sprinklers blasting from the ceiling quickly doused the remaining flames that had been crawling their way up her attacker's legs.

Shiloh's knees gave out, and she sank to the floor. It was over. It was finally over. Though her legs were shaking too badly to attempt to stand again, she crawled her way toward Samson.

"I'm coming, my friend," she croaked. *Please be okay.* Tears streamed from her eyes at the thought that he might be mortally wounded this time. All of her differences with him aside, he'd proven to be a loyal friend and battle buddy again and again and again.

His arms were clasped around her attacker's body in a bear-like hug. Sobbing, she reached for his wrist and found his pulse beating faintly. He was still alive, but just barely. She tucked her pistol back in her boot and reached for his limp hands, hoping to pull him away from the creep he'd tackled. The moment she lifted his arms, a new sound met her ears.

"Shiloh!" a man shouted hoarsely from somewhere nearby.

"Gabe!" she whispered, instantly recognizing his voice. *What are you doing here?* Still holding on to Samson's hands, she glanced over her shoulder.

It was a mistake. A hot, slimy hand slapped against her neck, and thick fingers slowly curled around her throat.

What the—? Oh, my lands! She'd forgotten the first rule of being a soldier. *Never let your guard down.*

Choking for air, she twisted from side to side in the effort to break free, but he held her neck firmly captive. The hand around her throat pulled her lower, one inch at a time, until her gaze was on the same level as the crazed eyes of the man in the gas mask. He said something garbled through the hose of his mask. It sounded eerily like, "You are mine."

"Shiloh!" Gabe's voice was closer this time. "Mercy!" he muttered as he fell to his knees beside her. His fist swung in an arc and connected to the side of her attacker's head.

Arrow Westfield's eyes closed, and the hand on her throat slid to the ground.

"The police are coming," Gabe assured in a voice that was hoarse from the smoke swirling around them. "I called Emmitt on my way here."

Shiloh tried to thank him for his timely appearance, but her voice wouldn't work. For one dizzy moment, she feared she'd conjured him up in her dreams, and that he wasn't really there at all.

Then her eyelids fluttered closed, and she slumped into the protective circle of his arms.

EPILOGUE

Two months later

Gabe laced his fingers through Shiloh's, glancing down every few seconds to make sure he wasn't dreaming. They were seated on the rear balcony of the Anderson Ranch B&B, in the same two-seater Adirondack bench where they'd begun their first date. He couldn't be happier to be in town again. Though his travel schedule remained jam-packed, he flew to town every chance he could, even if it was only for a day or two.

"You keep coming back," Shiloh noted softly.

They were overlooking one of the rear pastures, where a segment of Brody's famous herd was grazing. The sun was dipping on the horizon, trading in its earlier golden rays for the rosier hues of sunset. A dog barked in the distance, and a pair of ranch hands laughed somewhere below the balcony.

"I told you I would always come back, so long as you didn't give me a reason not to." Gabe raised her hand to his mouth and brushed a kiss against the top of her hand. He knew he was staring at her like a moron, but man! He couldn't seem to tear his gaze away. Her transformation was that breathtaking.

The shadows that had haunted her eyes since the day they'd met were finally gone. Her cheeks had filled out just enough to chase away the weary gauntness, and a wisp of her wavy blonde hair was blowing enticingly across her eyes.

He reached over to tuck it back behind her ear. His hand lingered against her cheek. Unless he was sorely mistaken, his smoking hot Marine was actually wearing makeup! And don't even get him started on her floral scoop-neck blouse and sassy white tennis skirt. Most importantly, the ugly finger smudges from her stalker's attack had finally faded from the soft skin of her neck.

"I didn't believe you at first. I wanted to, but..." She stopped and caught her breath at the way he dipped his head to gaze directly into her eyes. "I'm just a lowly little maid, and you're a big cheese country western singer and all." Her blue-gray eyes twinkled merrily at him.

"Whatever," he scoffed. Since he knew she was teasing, he didn't bother to reassure her that she was so much more than a maid. "I'll say it a different way, darling. I will always come back to you, because I love you. God is my anchor, but you're my compass always pointing me toward home."

"Gabe!" she cried in a tremulous voice. "That's so beautiful! You should totally put that line in one of your songs."

"Ha! In case you haven't figured it out yet, every song I've written in the last few months has been a love letter to you."

He dipped his head to claim her mouth in the tenderest of kisses. She'd given him every reason to come back to her, from her endless supply of sweet kisses to her fierce loyalty to her whispered words of love. Oh, and he'd finally found the perfect gift for her — a brand spanking new cell phone with a service plan of her own. Thank God she used it every day when they were apart to send him quick messages about what was happening in her part of the world. She also sent him dozens of selfies (at his specific request), in which she was usually doing something ridiculous like crossing her eyes or making fish lips at him.

Or hanging upside down from the back of a horse... Apparently Foster and Crew had gotten it inside their thick skulls that she would be the perfect candidate to train in the art of trick riding. *Think again, fellas.* Gabe had other plans for his sweetheart. Much better ones.

"I love you so much, Gabe," she sighed. "I'm kinda new at this relationship stuff, so maybe it's not cool to admit this, but I've really missed you."

"About that." He leaned in for another kiss, tickled to the moon and back that she'd missed him. There was no telling if she'd missed him half as much as he'd missed her. But hey! It wasn't a contest. "I have some ideas for how to fix this."

"Uh-oh." She chuckled. "You think we need fixing?"

"Not us. Just the distance between us."

"Well, what do you have in mind?" Her expression turned anxious. "You know I can't leave here yet. Shayley's baby isn't due for a few more weeks, and—"

He stopped her anxious tirade with a thumb against her lower lip. Tracing the soft rosy petal of it, he shared the big news he'd kept bottled up all day. "I didn't want to say anything until I was sure it was happening, but I've put a contract on a place here in the country."

Her eyes widened. "You're buying a house?"

"Exactly six point three miles down the road, darling. I'm still deciding if it makes sense to renovate the two-story that's already there, or tear it down and design something new. Either way, I'm going to have to construct a separate recording studio, so I can spend less time in Nashville and more time working from home." He drew a finger down her cheek. "Near a certain lovely singer who owns my heart."

"She sounds awesome," Shiloh teased. "You'll have to introduce us sometime."

Unable to resist, Gabe captured her sassy mouth in another very satisfying kiss.

Though her eyes were shining at his news, she rolled them the moment he lifted his head. "The fact that you even have options like that sorta blows my mind. Tearing houses down. Throwing new ones up. Don't forget you're talking to a gal who's probably spent more time sleeping under the open sky or inside of tents, than in a real bed."

"Well, if you'd like to toss down a tent on my property," he teased, "be my guest." Then he sobered. "But I actually had something a little more permanent in mind."

"Did you now, Mr. Romero?" She reached up to cup his face with both hands. "I was about to say yes to the tent. But, by all means, let's hear my other options."

"Marry me, Shiloh." He caught her gasp with his mouth, deepening their kiss to say the rest of what was on his heart without words. He'd planned to say something more romantic, to get on his knees, to flash a ring beneath her nose...but sometimes a bunch of extra words weren't needed.

He raised his head to meet her astonished gaze.

"Yes," she whispered so adoringly that he fell in love with her all over again.

That was his Shiloh. No games. Nothing but pure, heart-stopping honesty.

"How soon will you marry me?" he begged.

Though her eyes were misty and her cheeks

flushed a gorgeous shade of pink, she glanced down at her watch. "The night is young, Mr. Romero."

Now you're talking! He stood and gently tugged her to her feet.

"I was kidding, Gabe!"

"If I didn't happen to know the minister at the church down the road was on vacay," he warned tenderly.

"I don't have a wedding dress."

"Then wear whatcha got on, darling."

"Fine, but there's something else we should probably do first." She slid her arms around his neck.

"What's that?"

"I bet everyone on the ranch is down in the kitchen, wondering where we are and making up the most atrocious stories behind our backs."

"Your point?" He couldn't have cared less.

"Let's go set 'em straight." Her eyes twinkled with mischief.

He was delighted beyond belief to hear that she was ready to announce their engagement to the world. "I'll go down there and put up with the likes of Foster under one condition." He'd spent so much time in the last few months being jealous of the guy, that the sight of him still rubbed him the wrong way. Gabe knew he wasn't being fair. Foster had enough on his shoulders worrying about his brother, who was hanging on by a thread in the hospital. For Shiloh and Shayley's sake, Gabe was going to have to really make more of an effort to make nice with the youngest Kane.

"Oooo...a condition!" Shiloh looked fascinated. "By all means, lay it on me."

"I'll pay a visit to the kitchen with you, so long as you agree to make some music with me once we get there." Gabe was sort of dying to mingle his voice with hers again. It had been too long since the last time — more than a week, and that was only if he counted the time they'd sung a little jingle together over the phone.

Shiloh looked nervous. "I haven't practiced in days."

"That's okay, darling." He swung her in an impromptu dance. "No matter how long I'm away, we always seem to be in perfect tune each time I return."

"I guess we're about to find out." As she danced with him toward the door leading inside, she let out a peal of laughter. And it was more beautiful to him than any music he'd ever composed.

———

Like this book? Leave a review now!

Join Jo's List and never miss a new release or a great sale on her books.

Want to find out how Foster Kane REALLY feels about Shayley Neeson and the way his older brother has been

treating her? Keep turning the page for a sneak peek at
Born In Texas, Book #4: DAMAGED HERO
right now!

*Can't get enough of Jo's sweet hero romance stories? Check out **The Rebound Rescue** — her first title in the bestselling DISASTER CITY SEARCH & RESCUE SERIES.*
When an ex-bodybuilder (recovering from a broken heart) throws himself wholeheartedly into search and rescue operations, while a genius research scientist plots to redirect some of his hunky attention to her...

Much love,
Jo

SNEAK PREVIEW: DAMAGED HERO

He has a checkered past to overcome. She has a baby on the way. When tragedy strikes, all they have left to cling to is God...and each other!

Foster Kane is an all-in kinda guy. He's partied hard, spent a few years in the pen, and is now working like crazy to make up for past wrong. After he lands a job at Anderson Ranch, things are finally looking up. But his older brother is home from the Marines so messed up in the head that he can barely take care of himself, much less his new wife and the baby they have on the way. Foster steps in to help and soon finds his loyalties torn between his brother and the spirited mother-to-be his brother never got around to legally marrying.

Shayley Neeson is a penniless orphan, raised by an older sister who eventually left her, too, when she enlisted in the Marines. And now she's married to one of her sister's comrades-in-arms who claims a piece of paper won't make them any more married. The only person she's ever been able to count on — no matter what — is her rebel brother-in-law. A guy everyone else thinks is damaged...

When danger comes knocking, Foster proves yet again that he's the one constant in Shayley's life, but will he ever be more? Does a love triangle like theirs stand a chance at leading to a happily-ever-after? Can anything beautiful or good ever come from so much brokenness?

★*BORN IN TEXAS is a series of sweet and inspirational, standalone romantic suspense stories about small town, everyday heroes. WARNING: Lots of heart, plenty of humor, and always a happily-ever-after!*

———

Damaged Hero

Coming September, 2021 to eBook, paperback, and Kindle Unlimited!

The whole alphabet is coming! Read them all:
A - Accidental Hero
B - Best Friend Hero
C - Celebrity Hero
D - Damaged Hero
E - Enemies to Hero

Much love,
Jo

SNEAK PREVIEW: THE BRIDESMAID RESCUE

Late June

I'm in serious trouble. At least Emma Taylor's heart was. It was speeding like a sprint car around a racetrack at the way the tall, dark Marine was gazing at her. *What is wrong with me?* Maybe she was tired, or maybe she hadn't chugged enough coffee this morning, because an encounter with a fellow soldier never had this effect on her. Not once in her eight years of service to the U.S. Marines, anyway.

As a military police officer deployed to Afghanistan, she was accustomed to dealing with hundreds of soldiers every day. Sometimes thousands. So what was so special about this one? She didn't even know the guy's name. Not that she couldn't take a quick peek at his name tag after she and her police dog, Scout, finished circling his Humvee.

Beneath her lashes, she noted that the Marine was standing back the appropriate dozen feet or so, giving her and her K9 partner the space they required to inspect his vehicle in the crowded middle lane of the checkpoint. He wasn't hovering over her in that annoying way some soldiers did, as if standing closer to a police officer somehow provided them with an extra measure of security in this God-forsaken corner of the world.

The truth was, she was just as exposed to a stray missile as anyone else. The nine millimeter caliber pistol strapped inside her holster didn't have the faintest hope of protecting her from the blast of a bomb or a grenade. Nope. Her safety rested squarely in the hands of the very soldiers whose long lines of vehicles she was currently processing.

Their fire power and bravery was all that stood between the checkpoint she helped run and the enemy lines they would be heading toward next. Her MP station would serve as their last stop before they headed south to Kandahar — into the heart of enemy territory.

As Emma worked, she tried not to think about the dangers that the handsome Marine and his comrades would soon be facing. She'd learned a long time ago to just do her job. Her personal rules for maintaining her sanity during war were simple: Don't memorize names. Don't try to remember faces. Don't get too attached. Most of these guys (along with the handful of gals in their ranks) she would never see again.

That was a good thing, because she wouldn't ever have to know which ones made it home in one piece and which ones would be returned in a box. Well, normally it was a good thing not to know stuff like that, but she suddenly found herself breaking one of her personal rules and wishing like crazy that one Marine in particular would, in fact, make it home safely.

"Any chance you can shed some light on what you and your dog are looking for, Officer Taylor?"

Emma blinked as the tall Black man in question strode across the lane in her direction. Gosh, but he was swoony! All broad and ripped beneath his sand-colored camouflage uniform. The morning rays beat down on his sun-kissed features, accentuating the angle of his jaw and his squared-off chin. The brim of his hat was pulled just low enough over his eyes that it was hard to read his expression. He sounded Texan, but she was guessing he also had some island blood in him.

"Who says we're looking for anything, Sergeant..." Emma allowed her gaze to drop to his name tape. "Zane." *Wow!* A name with a Z. His last name was as gorgeous as the rest of him.

Her heartbeat sped at his nearness. There was just so much of him, though it wasn't merely his size affecting her senses. It was something more — a special brand of awareness zinging between them. She wondered again what was wrong with her this morning. *No emotional strings. Just do your job, Emma. You're not his wife, fiancée, or girlfriend.* But there was a part of her that wished she was. Or at least something more to him than a random MP at a random checkpoint.

"I do, ma'am." He was close enough for her to see his eyes now. His dark, coffee-brew gaze swept her face and instantly registered male admiration. "You've circled my vehicle three times already."

"Did I?" she pretended innocence, trying to sound offhand. "Guess I like to be thorough, sergeant."

"Marcus," he corrected without missing a beat. "Marcus Zane. So did I pass the test, or are you about to whip out your cuffs?" His lips twisted into a half-smile, and his baritone drawl held a note of humor. However, there was a no-nonsense look in his eyes that told her he very much understood the dangers he would soon be facing.

She chuckled, liking how smoothly he'd slipped

his first name into the conversation. It wasn't necessary for her to know it, but she was every shade of thrilled to realize that he wanted her to. "Aw, are you flirting with me, sergeant?" She lowered her voice so that none of the other soldiers milling around could hear her words.

"We're at war, ma'am," he shot back, pressing a hand to his chest in mock indignation. "Sorry, but there's no time to flirt with a beautiful woman."

You think I'm beautiful, huh? She felt a wave of warmth travel across her cheeks that had nothing to do with the desert heat radiating off the sand surrounding them. "Thank you." She let out the breath she'd been holding. "You wouldn't believe the offers I get sometimes." Or the desperate pleadings from a few very young, very cocky, very scared soldiers right before they crossed into enemy territory. She'd been proposed to at least a dozen times this week already, by men desperate to have a reason for Divine Providence to keep them alive in the coming days.

"Oh, I probably would." He snorted. "I've spent enough years working around dudes. Not to mention, I happen to be one, myself."

"I noticed," she returned dryly.

"Good. Mission accomplished." Ignoring Scout's warning growl, he fell into step beside her.

Though Emma had already mentally cleared both Sergeant Zane and his vehicle for moving on, she couldn't see any harm in detaining him a few minutes longer by making a fourth pass around his Humvee. His unit wasn't scheduled to depart for another hour, and neither of them was in a hurry to end their flirt session. That's what it was. There was no point in lying to herself.

He dipped his dark head closer to hers, ignoring another growl from Scout. "Since you dodged my first question, I don't suppose the extra attention you're giving me and my men has anything to do with the very important package we're transporting?"

She glanced up in surprise, no longer pretending to inspect his vehicle. "You know about the package?" The prisoner his unit was escorting was in the central Humvee, three vehicles back from his. His situation was highly classified, so she doubted many soldiers in his unit had received the full briefing on the man's identity or the reason he was being transported.

Marcus Zane's dark brows shot up. He gave a low whistle. "I do now, Officer Taylor. I had my suspicions before, but..."

"Emma," she interrupted, hoping to distract him from his bulldog pursuit of details about their prisoner. "And you can quit pretending that I just made a major slip-up, in the hopes of wheedling more information out of me. It's one of those need-to-know things. I don't make the rules." Her gut told her that he not only needed to know, but that he already knew. His adept way at maneuvering their conversation was more about establishing common ground between them, and quickly, since he had less than an hour to spare. Kind of genius, actually. And wildly flattering.

"Emma," he repeated softly. His dark gaze roved over her face again. "I'm really glad you decided your name was on my list of need-to-know items. I like it, by the way. It suits you."

He didn't offer any of the cheesy compliments she was accustomed to receiving. Just a simple *I like it*. Her insides melted a few more degrees at the genuine note in his voice. "Nice to know," she teased, "since I'm sorta stuck with it."

"So..." He canted his broad frame in her direction, eliciting a third, damp-sounding snarl from Scout.

She tugged the agitated German Shepherd back a few inches and gave him the signal to heel.

"Now, who's flirting?" Marcus teased, eyeing her movements. "You just ordered your dog not to devour me, didn't you?"

"Something like that." She smiled sadly as she glanced around them, taking in the serious expressions on the faces of his comrades. "Unfortunately, this isn't a breakfast date, and I don't see a napkin to scrawl my phone number on." He was shipping out in a matter of minutes.

"That's alright. I have a very good memory and no plans to forget you." His gaze caressed hers. It felt as intimate as if their hands had touched.

"What are you doing?" she whispered, hating the fact that she was blushing and hoping no one was watching them too closely.

"With your permission, I'd like to kiss you inside my head before I go."

Her lips parted on a breathy chuckle. "Most guys don't ask for permission before imagining themselves doing far more than that." Not all that surprising, considering how few females there were around.

"Yeah, well, I happen to have higher standards than that," he returned in his lazy drawl. "Much higher. In fact, I'm only going to kiss you if you agree to kiss me back."

What? She gave another breathless laugh but didn't drop her gaze from his. They shared a highly charged, heart-racing moment.

"And only after you recite your phone number, so I can memorize it."

She shook her head at him, her smile widening. He had to know her cell phone wouldn't work on this side of the world. It wasn't going to work until she returned stateside, which could be months from now.

In a soft voice hitched with emotion, she quickly rattled off her number.

He bent his head over hers, canting it slightly as if he was swooping in for a kiss, but he stopped several inches away. "This is the part where you kiss me back, Emma Taylor."

He never touched her. He didn't close his eyes, either, but she felt thoroughly kissed after he raised his head. "So am I the first Black guy you've ever necked with?"

She gasped at the brazen question. "Does it

matter?" No, she'd never dated a Black guy before. Then again, she hadn't done much dating since high school. Between boot camp, MP training, dog handler school, and deployments, there hadn't been time for exploring many personal relationships. Or maybe she just hadn't met the right guy. Until now.

"To me it does. I want to be your first."

"Marcus," she whispered in an agonized voice, knowing she'd let things go far enough between them. She'd already broken every single one of her personal rules about getting too close to a fellow soldier.

"And your last," he added swiftly, dipping his head to gaze deeply into her eyes. "In case you're wondering, I'm gunning for the spot as the *only* guy in your life."

A shaky sound of mirth escaped her. "Poor Dad." *Don't do this, Marcus.* What he was about to face in battle would be hard enough. He didn't need her as a distraction inside his head.

Marcus snickered. "Maybe he and I can work something out." He made a face. "I get ninety-nine percent of your attention. He gets a solid one percent."

"You're going to have to do better than that," she confessed shyly. "I'm an only child, so he's very territorial." And that was putting it mildly. Dad had always been her biggest and loudest cheerleader, her unwavering supporter of everything she tried — though he was no more thrilled about her decision to join the military than her lifelong circle of friends had been.

"Fine! Two percent to my ninety-eight. You drive a hard bargain, woman." His teasing baritone resonated deliciously through her.

Though she smiled again, her thoughts were already leaping ahead to reality. "I wish you the best, Marcus. I truly do. With whatever lovely gal you end up with." She knew they weren't likely to see each other again.

"Thank you," he retorted cheerfully. "Is that a challenge, beautiful?"

"No, it's..." She sighed. *Goodbye.*

"I'm going to call you, Emma." He expression grew serious as he mimed the act of lifting a phone to his ear. "Your number is permanently seared into my memory. Promise. I just can't tell you exactly when."

And now he was making promises he probably wouldn't be able to keep.

"It's been really nice meeting you, Marcus." For some reason, she couldn't bring herself to tell him goodbye. It sounded too foreboding, considering their current circumstances. Too final.

His upper lip curled. "I can do better than nice. Just wait until I follow up that kiss inside my head with the hands-on version."

Okay, now I'm swooning on the inside. "A real one next time, huh?" she teased. Did he seriously envision a next time between them? It was preposterous and slightly insane to consider their brief encounter the start of something, but golly! He wasn't kidding. It sure felt like something, virtual kiss and all.

"I'd prefer to call it our second kiss. I think we both know the first one already happened."

She pursed her lips and pretended to consider his words. "On a scale of one to ten in the romance department, it wasn't too shabby."

"Oh, now you're judging me?" His dark gaze turned wicked.

"That's what you wanted, you cocky Texan." She playfully waggled a finger at him. "Don't bother trying to deny it. You wanted my attention, Marcus Zane, and you got it."

He looked so self-satisfied that she laughed again. "I hope that means you believe I'm going to call you?"

She made a face and glanced away. "I've never been a wait-beside-the-phone kinda gal. I'm more of grab-life-by-the-horns kinda peep."

His voice dropped to a lower, huskier tenor. "Our next kiss will be the kind that's worth waiting for. Trust me."

Her mouth went dry as her head spun back to his. "What makes you so sure?"

"I just know, Emma. One look at you. That's all it took."

The way he was looking at her now was doing ridiculous things to her heart. Things neither of them had any business feeling on a sandy road facing Kandahar.

She gave him a measuring look, foolishly wanting

to believe the fairytale promise he was trying to hand her. "How about we make a deal? You call me, and I'll believe you then. No more doubts. No more questions."

"I will." He started to give her a two-fingered salute, but a male whoop of joy made him pause.

———

Hope you enjoyed the excerpt from
DISASTER CITY SEARCH AND RESCUE:
The Bridesmaid Rescue
Available now on Amazon + FREE in KU!

Other Jo Grafford books in this series:
The Rebound One Rescue
The Fake Bride Rescue
The Blind Date Rescue
The Secret Baby Rescue
The Bridesmaid Rescue
The Girl Next Door Rescue
The Secret Crush Rescue
The Bachelorette Rescue
The Maid by Mistake Rescue
The Unlucky Bride Rescue

Much love,
Jo

SNEAK PREVIEW: WINDS OF CHANGE

Heart Lake

She's home.

Josh Hawling had always known this day would come...eventually. He watched the Gulfstream catch the sun and gleam like white fire as it banked left and circled around for its final descent to the narrow landing strip. A few mountain gusts rocked the aircraft, but the pilot expertly steered through them. He nosed downward and touched the landing wheels to the tarmac. Throwing the engine thrusters in reverse and raising the wing spoilers, he swiftly reduced his speed and rolled to a stop.

Hope Remington was finally back in Texas, where she belonged.

"She's been gone ten years." Mr. Elmer Remington, superintendent of the Heart Lake School District, eagerly regarded the airplane on the other side of the glass. Indulgent pride radiated from his lined features. He'd come straight from the district office in his business suit, but his straw Stetson and leather boots underscored the fact that he was and always would be a rancher first. "Her return is nothing short of a miracle."

By a miracle, Josh knew Mr. Remington was referring to the fact that he'd negotiated long and hard with his fellow school board members to tweak a few of the job requirements in her favor. He'd wanted to hire a hometown girl as the next head principal of Heart Lake High, but Hope wouldn't have stood a chance in the interview if the powers-that-be hadn't waved the prior experience requirement. The ink was still drying on her PhD, and she'd only served as an assistant principal so far. This was the first time she would be running an entire high school on her own.

Josh was concerned about how much responsibility the school board was placing on her shoulders this early in her career. However, no one had asked for his opinion on the matter, so he was keeping it to himself. For now.

He was simply the guy they'd hired to protect her — off the record, of course. On paper, his security team was actually under contract to guard the student body and school facilities as a whole. Not one person, specifically. The sidebar agreement for Josh to stick as close to Hope as a cocklebur had

happened in a closed-door meeting with the superintendent, alone. Though the older gentleman was only
distantly related to Hope — a cousin of her grandpar-
ents twice removed — he'd always considered her to
be family.

The door to the gleaming white Gulfstream
opened, and a set of equally gleaming white metal
stairs descended. A red high-heeled boot appeared
next. It was soon followed by the rest of the woman
Josh had waited so long to see again. Her long, blonde
hair was draped over one shoulder, cascading nearly
to the waist of her sassy denim dress. She wasn't as
tanned as she used to be, probably because of the
number of hours she was required to spend indoors
these days. But she still had her impetuous smile and
walked with the same energy and confidence of the
barrel racing, rodeo queen he remembered.

Though Josh didn't so much as flinch, it felt like a
sucker punch in the gut to watch Hope Remington
walk down the jet stairs and move across the pave-
ment to the airline terminal. Toward him, instead of
away from him, for the first time in ten years.

Only a single wall of glass separated them now. He
and the district superintendent had been awaiting her
arrival from the other side of it. Though Josh sorely
doubted Hope would appreciate his presence, Mr.
Remington had insisted he be included in her
welcome party. Then again, she'd moved on with her
life years ago. Maybe she'd long since forgiven and
forgotten his past sins. There was a distinct possi-

bility she wouldn't even recognize the older version of him. He was a good four inches taller than the last time they'd been together — bigger, broader, and wiser. *Infinitely* wiser. A man who'd learned from his mistakes and had no interest in repeating them.

There was no way she'd be feeling even half of what he was feeling when she finally laid eyes on him and realized who he was — pain laced with bitter longing over the way he'd left things between them. Of all the things he'd left unsaid and even worse, the things he'd left undone. Especially the way he'd failed to meet her at their favorite rendezvous and run off to college together, like the lovesick fools they'd once been.

She'd been a slender teenager at the time, full of dreams and plans that were bigger than him, anxious to leave their small town existence behind and explore the world in ways only a Remington could afford to do. She was a grown woman with big city polish now, one who'd tasted and experienced the globe from Anchorage, to Amsterdam, to Paris. Yeah, he'd followed her adventures by lurking on her social media accounts, since she'd never bothered kicking him off. His lurking had also kept him painfully informed about her social life. There'd been pictures of all the places she'd visited and all the friends she'd made along the way. Guy friends. Lots of guy friends. He wondered how many of them she'd dated.

Those pictures were the only reason Josh knew that the auburn-haired man striding at her side in a designer gray suit was more than her pilot. He was one of her closest friends, possibly her boyfriend. A billionaire philanthropist from Alaska, who was supposedly coming to help clear the tornado damage in Heart Lake by financing a number of their restoration projects — the first and biggest project being the overhaul of their disaster planning and preparedness infrastructure.

But Josh wasn't buying the guy's story. He could think of only one reason why a man of Kellan Maddox's elite connections and financial resources would travel to such a small, rural town, and that was to pursue the heart of the woman Josh had never stopped loving.

Well, Mr. Money Bags was in for one heck of a surprise when he discovered the competition he would be going up against.

Me.

Josh pulled his Stetson low over his eyes as the gate door flew open, and Hope stepped inside the terminal. He preferred not to be recognized right away. He'd rather witness her unrehearsed reaction to the sight of him when she finally realized who he was.

Her expressive blue gaze scanned the small waiting area and quickly lit on Mr. Remington.

"Elmer!" she cried joyfully.

Josh experienced a familiar jolt at the sound of her voice. It was all he could do not to step forward and sweep her into his arms as she moved in their direction. She hurried forward with her hands outstretched. Not to him, unfortunately.

Mr. Remington eagerly took her slender hands in his. "Welcome home, Hope." He leaned in to kiss her cheek. "We couldn't be happier that you've agreed to join our staff at Heart Lake High."

She gave his wrinkled hands an affectionate squeeze back before dropping them. "How could I say no to such a kind and generous offer? There certainly aren't many twenty-nine-year-old administrators out there getting this kind of opportunity handed to them."

The superintendent nodded sagely.

Her smile widened to a full blast of warmth and humor. "I probably don't want to know how many arms you twisted or favors you called in to make this happen."

"You're the right person for the job, Hope," he assured quickly. "Don't you ever doubt it. It's the only reason I reached out and asked you to apply."

"I'm so glad you did," she murmured. Her smile dimmed a few degrees, as her gaze became washed with nostalgia. "As soon as I heard about the storm damage, I knew I needed to come home."

"Don't thank me yet." Mr. Remington grimaced. "Combining two high school campuses isn't exactly going to be a stroll around the lake."

"I understand what needs to be done, sir." She met his gaze soberly. "That's why it had to be me, isn't it?"

"Yes."

Josh knew what they were leaving unsaid. Hope was a hometown girl. An insider, despite all the years she'd been gone. She was one of the few people in the county who stood a chance at maneuvering her way through the politics, family feuds, and old grudges that fueled everything that took place in their small mountain town. She'd grown up in the middle of those politics. She'd been an integral part of them. Only time would tell how much of them remained in her, how they would fuel her plans and drive her decisions.

Elmer Remington and his school board were banking on the fact that her decisions in the coming days would drive their high school in the right direction, toward a unity that the students from the north and south sides of town had never before tasted. They'd been arch rivals for years. Putting them under one roof for the first time was a lofty goal at best, a foolish one at worst.

In that moment, Hope's natty airline pilot strode over to join their group. Up until now, he'd been conferring with the gate attendant, signing paperwork and such. He held out a hand to the superintendent. "I'm Kellan Maddox. You must be the Elmer Remington I've heard so much about."

Josh's upper lip curled at the ruby signet ring riding the man's pinky finger, along with the diamonds glinting from his cufflinks. *What a pretty boy!* If this was the kind of man that revved Hope's motor these days, then she'd changed in ways Josh had never considered her capable of changing. Lifting his jaw a fraction, he drilled her with a curious stare while the two men shook hands.

Without preamble, Mr. Remington dropped Pretty Boy's hand and turned in Josh's direction. "Hope, I reckon you remember Josh Hawling? He'll be serving as our security director at Heart Lake High."

At the mention of his name, her slender shoulders seemed to freeze. However, the smile she sent in his direction sparkled with the same cheery carelessness as it had upon her arrival.

"Josh Hawling? You're kidding!"

He tested her bland response by thrusting out one large, callused paw. *Stick your hand in it, lady, and I'll show you who's not kidding.*

After a moment of hesitation, she pressed her fingers lightly against his. It was far from a real hand-shake; he had no intention of letting her get away with such a half-hearted gesture.

"It's good to see you again, Hope." Josh closed his hand around her highfalutin one with its perfect manicure and gave it a full cowboy squeeze. *Hate me all you want, darlin'. I deserve it.* But saw no point in pretending they didn't have history between them. No, he wasn't going to make a scene in front of her filthy rich boyfriend. But she was going to acknowledge, at least to him, that they'd once meant something to each other.

Her lips parted as she stared at their joined hands. Once upon a time, that kind of handshake would've been followed by a quick tug closer so he could plant a firm, hard kiss on her. He could tell from the momentary flash of distress in her gaze that she was remembering.

Good. He kept her hand ensconced in his a little longer than polite manners deemed necessary before letting it go. He was satisfied that he'd made his point.

Something flickered in her gaze. Something real and potent. Something angry and wild. She quickly squashed it and schooled her expression, but it was too late. He'd already seen it.

There you are. Feeling like he'd stayed on top of a bucking bull a good second longer than it took to qualify for the next round, he transferred his attention to the fancy creature at her side, inwardly daring him to stick out his pinky ring one last time. *I will break your hand, Pretty Boy. I will crush you.*

Surprise stained the man's aquiline features as he met Josh's sneer. "So, ah…I look forward to sitting down with you and your team, Mr. Hawling." To his credit, he made no move to shake Josh's hand. "Considering the line of business you're in, I wouldn't mind getting your input on the emergency sound systems we're looking to install here in Heart Lake."

It took a few extra seconds for the claws of jealousy to uncurl enough from Josh's ribcage to process what the man was saying. "I'd be glad to share my thoughts with you, Mr. Maddox." *On a few key things, in particular.* He reached inside his vest pocket to produce a business card for Lonestar Security. He and his partner, Decker Kingston, a guy from Houston that he'd met on the rodeo circuit, had opened shop inside a cheap storage locker about five years ago. However, their business had taken off to the point where they now had security personnel working in every mountain town in a hundred-mile radius, and a few cities farther away than that. Oh, and they owned a real home office nowadays, right smack in the center of downtown Heart Lake. Big and new with a nice view of the water.

"Thanks. I'll be in touch." He pocketed the card in the pocket of his trousers. Italian silk, if Josh wasn't mistaken. The only reason he knew that ridiculous fact was due to being sized for a tux to wear at the upcoming wedding of a friend in the police department, Lincoln Hudson. Josh would've never wasted his hard-earned money on something as frivolous as Italian silk. His own wardrobe hadn't changed much over the years. Even though his championship bull riding days were over, it was still jeans and boots for him, thank you very much.

"Oh, and my friends call me Kellan." The man's humor-infused gaze met his knowingly, as he stepped closer to Hope.

Clever. Josh eyed the man's movements, wondering if he'd be fool enough to touch her while Josh was watching them. He stared the guy down, delighted by the fact he towered a good two inches over him, maybe three.

"My friends call me Lucky Ten." It was because of how many seconds he'd stayed on the bull that had won him his final championship pot. It was the same bull that had snapped three of his ribs and nearly broken his neck in the time he'd managed to remain seated on his viciously twisting flanks.

Elmer Remington gave a chortle of pride as he reached up to clap Josh on the shoulder. "That lucky ten seconds sure put our small town on the map," he chortled. "Got this fella's name in the Bull Riding Hall of Fame, too."

"I'm sorry I missed it," Hope cut in. Though her words were gracious, her tone was as chilly as a cone of shaved ice at a county fair. "Unfortunately, my college studies didn't leave much time for rodeo hopping and partying."

Rodeo Hopping? Partying? Josh arched an eyebrow at her. *Darling, while you were busy toting around pretty pink backpacks and tennis rackets, I was busy making bank and saving your...*

His brain froze as she reached for Kellan Maddox's hand. *Oh, for the love of—!* He glanced away, unable to bear the way she tipped her face up to her new billionaire boyfriend. It was too painfully reminiscent of the way she used to look at him.

It was beginning to look like his secret agreement to serve as Hope Remington's personal bodyguard was going to be a heck of a lot harder assignment than he'd bargained for.

———

"Don't," Kellan whispered in Hope's ear. He gave her hand a friendly squeeze before letting it go and taking a safe step away from her. There was a sheen of sadness in his turquoise gaze that she'd never seen before. There was a mild glint of accusation there, too, and disappointment.

Remorse slammed into her at the realization that the emotional slap she'd intended for the stone-hearted Josh Hawling had landed entirely on the wrong guy. She stared at Kellan in dismay, a thousand apologies burning on her lips. He'd been so sweetly supportive of her during her recent lineup of inter-views and her subsequent decision to leave Alaska to accept the job offer in Texas.

And there was no way he'd decided to open the magnanimous pockets of the Black Ties charity foun-dation to rebuild her hometown out of sheer benevo-lence. He'd done it for her, for their friendship, which she'd suspected for some time now that he was plan-ning to turn into something more. For a friendship that she'd just inadvertently finished giving a careless stomp.

Wanting more than anything to repair the damage, she reached out to touch his arm. "If you'll excuse us for a quick minute, Kellan and I need to collect our luggage. How about we meet outside in, say..." She scanned Elmer Remington's features in a desperate plea for him to save the rapidly deteriorating situation.

"Five or ten minutes would be great." His gaze dropped to the hand she had resting on Kellan's arm and festered with something akin to rebuke. "Josh brought us here in one of his security vehicles. We'll bring it around front." He made a comical face. "Assuming you're not bringing all of your household belongings on the first trip, it should be roomy enough to hold us all."

Cute. She forced a soft chuckle. "I only brought a few suitcases, my friend. Everything else will arrive on the moving truck."

"Perfect. We'll see you in a few, then."

She nodded. "I'm looking forward to our upcoming tour of central office and Heart Lake High. Thank you for making all these arrangements, Elmer, and on such short notice, too." The new school year would begin in two short weeks. There was no time to waste.

"You betcha, kid. Ahem." He pretended to clear his throat as he raised his bushy gray brows in askance. "I reckon I should be addressing you as Dr. Remington these days?"

"Don't you dare!" Relief infused her over the fact that he didn't seem inclined to hold her misstep with her new security director against her. Risking a glance in the blasted man's direction, she found Josh's dark gaze resting on her in grim resolution.

He was back in control of his anger, but just barely. So was she. Blinking at him in indignation, she silently upbraided him. *How dare you two-step your way back into my life like this without so much as a warning?* She lifted her chin as their gazes clashed. She could almost feel the sizzle between his scalding coffee brew eyes and her icy blue ones. *You have no right. Not anymore. You forfeited every privilege you had the day you stood me up at the bridge.*

Pivoting to follow after Kellan, who was already a few strides across the terminal, she finished the rest of her inner tirade. *You gave up everything the day you broke my heart, Josh Hawling!*

Kellan was still wearing his benign smile when she caught up to him.

"I'm so sorry about what happened back there." Her voice was tremulous with remorse as they faced the baggage carousel together. The first suitcases were just now popping past the rubber flap in the wall and rotating their way on the conveyer belt.

"We're good, Hope." His hands were loosely resting on the tops of his trouser pockets. "It's not like you've ever been anything less than honest about the feelings you've never had for me," he sighed. "Now I know why."

"Oh, my lands, Kellan! It's not like that," she protested, needing him to understand that she hadn't been feeding him false hope in her direction. She valued their friendship enormously. His thoughts and opinions mattered to her. *He* mattered to her. "There is nothing, and I mean nothing, between Josh Hawling and me." *Not anymore.* "I honestly haven't laid eyes on the guy in over ten years."

"And yet it's pretty obvious that there *was* something between the two of you at some point." Kellan reached for her pair of red leather suitcases and set them on the floor between them. "Please don't try to deny it. The tension between you and him back there was, well, pretty intense."

"Was. Past tense." She pressed a hand against her racing heart. "There hasn't been so much as a single word between us since I left home."

"Interesting. You know what that tells me, Hope?"

She clasped her hands beneath her chin, beseeching him to believe her. "That your friendship means the world to me? And that I would never, ever, ever purposefully do anything to hurt you or it."

"Of course you wouldn't!" he exploded. Turning his back on the conveyer belt, he held out his arms to her. "Come here, you."

She flung her arms around him, hugging him tightly. "I don't ever want to lose you, Kellan."

"You're not going to." He pressed his cheek against hers. "I meant it when I said we're good, you and I. Just promise me one thing."

"Anything," she murmured damply.

He loosened his grasp to hold her at arm's length.

"Don't use me as a baseball bat to take any more whacks at your ex."

"I never intended for it to come across like that." She and Kellan had held hands before. They'd even gone on a few dates.

"He's a big dude, and I'm pretty sure he's already imagining all the ways he'd like to terminate my existence. He doesn't need any new inspiration, like the sight of you pretending to flirt with me."

"Seriously?" Hope dropped her arms and stepped back. "Since when did flirting become a crime in your book? You, of all people! You've probably dated every single female in Anchorage, myself included."

He shrugged. "Let's just say I prefer to date women who are emotionally available, as well."

She gave a gasp of protest. "I'm—"

"Not." He reached over to lightly tap her nose. "At least not right now. I'm not saying no or never to us, Hope, because I sure wouldn't mind another chance with you, at some point." He angled his head toward the door. "But you're going to need to resolve whatever unfinished business you have with Mr. Champion Bull Rider before we can do that."

"There's not anything to resolve." Hope closed her eyes while she dabbed at the damp corners of them. "He made that disastrously clear when we were supposed to leave town together, and he failed to show up."

"Ouch!" Kellan sharply pivoted in his brown leather wingtips to grab his own two suitcases. "He doesn't impress me as being that kind of a fool, but okay. Everyone makes mistakes."

"You think he made a mistake when he broke my heart?" She gave a sniff of disbelief. "Just a mistake, huh?" *No biggie.* "Gee, thanks."

"I do." Kellan waved over a baggage porter with a cart to load their suitcases. "So does he, apparently. From how butt sore your bull rider was acting back there, I'm betting he considers losing you to be the single biggest mistake of his life."

My bull rider? Mine? Uh, not any longer. But the humorous understanding in Kellan's voice tugged at Hope's overwrought emotions, bringing her dangerously close to tears again. "I wouldn't even know how to start a conversation like that with him." She shook her head, drawing her lower lip between her teeth. "Honestly? If I'd have known Josh Hawling and I were going to be forced to work together like this, I would have never accepted the job."

"Good to know." Josh's rumbly baritone announced from somewhere behind her.

When Hope spun in his direction, he treated her to a chilly smile. "Elmer sent me back in here to see what was taking so long. So what's it going to be, Dr. Remington?" He tipped his Stetson mockingly at her. "My vehicle, or should I direct your porter to take your suitcases back to the airplane?"

She stared back in growing fury. Yes, it was poor manners on her part to talk about him behind his back, but there was no reason to sneak up on her like this to eavesdrop, either. "How about you let Elmer know I've decided to call my own cab?" She hated the way Josh was smirking at her and wished, more than anything, he didn't have to look so crazy good looking in his distressed jeans and scuffed boots. Gosh, what was it about the guy that had always drawn her to him? He was like a dangerous infection, for pity's sake, a life-threatening one that she needed to carve out of her system, once and for all, before it destroyed her!

Studying her a moment longer, Josh waved their baggage porter toward the glass doors at the front of the terminal. "We didn't have a cab service in Heart Lake when you first left town, and the one that started up a few months ago was leveled by the tornado. So I'm your best bet for a ride to central office, princess. That is, unless you prefer to walk."

Princess? Really? She didn't think it was possible for a person to infuse more sarcasm in a single word. *No, I don't prefer to walk, you smug-faced jerk!* Without answering, she motioned her intention to Kellan to leave the building. Then she glided ahead of both men to the doors.

Josh somehow managed to arrive ahead of her to hold one of them open. "After you, Dr. Remington." He shot her another one of his maddening half grins that made her see red.

———

Hope you enjoyed the sneak preview of
HEART LAKE #1: Winds of Change
Available in eBook, paperback, and hard cover on Amazon
+ FREE in Kindle Unlimited!

Much love,
Jo

SNEAK PREVIEW: HER BILLIONAIRE BOSS

A demanding billionaire boss, a marriage of convenience, and a surprise baby...

Jacey Maddox is determined to atone for her forbidden love and tragically short marriage by dedicating the rest of her career to her late husband's family firm, Genesis & Sons. That is, if they'll consider hiring a hated Maddox...

CEO Luca Calcagni is determined to teach the rebel youngest daughter of their biggest rival the lesson of her life by hiring her as his personal assistant. He never counted on rekindling his former explosive attraction to her, any more than she counted on discovering she's carrying his late brother's baby. When she threatens to leave town and move as far as possible from the reaches of their decades-old family feud, it'll take his most skillful negotiating to maneuver her into a marriage of convenience to keep her and his last tie to his brother – her unborn child – in his life.

Except marriage to the stunningly beautiful, artistic, and complex Jacey turns out to be anything but convenient... He tries to convince himself it's only about revenge, but he can't help wondering (and secretly hoping) if her agreement to be his temporary wife could turn into his second chance at love with the only woman he's never been able to resist!

––––––

Her Billionaire Boss
Available in eBook, paperback, and Kindle Unlimited!

BLACK TIE BILLIONAIRES SERIES
Read them all!
Her Billionaire Boss
Her Billionaire Bodyguard
Her Billionaire Secret Admirer

Her Billionaire Best Friend
Her Billionaire Geek
Her Billionaire Double Date

Much love,
Jo

READ MORE JO

Jo is an Amazon bestselling author of sweet and inspirational romance stories with humor, heart, and happily-ever-afters.

Free Book!

Visit www.JoGrafford.com to sign up for Jo's New Release Newsletter and receive a FREE copy of one of her sweet romance stories!

1.) Follow on Amazon!
amazon.com/author/jografford

2.) Join Cuppa Jo Readers!
https://www.facebook.com/groups/CuppaJoReaders

3.) Join Heroes and Hunks Readers!

https://www.facebook.com/groups/HeroesandHunks/

4.) Follow on Bookbub!

https://www.bookbub.com/authors/jo-grafford

5.) Follow on Instagram!

https://www.instagram.com/jografford/

amazon.com/authors/jo-grafford

bookbub.com/authors/jo-grafford

facebook.com/jografford

twitter.com/jografford

instagram.com/jografford

pinterest.com/jografford

ALSO BY JO GRAFFORD

Visit www.JoGrafford.com to sign up for Jo's New Release Newsletter and to receive your FREE copy of one of her sweet romance stories!

———

Born In Texas: Hometown Heroes A-Z

written exclusively by Jo Grafford

The whole alphabet is coming!

A - Accidental Hero

B - Best Friend Hero

C - Celebrity Hero

D - Damaged Hero

E - Enemies to Hero

———

Disaster City Search and Rescue

(a multi-author series)

Titles by Jo:

The Rebound Rescue

The Plus One Rescue

The Blind Date Rescue

The Fake Bride Rescue

The Secret Baby Rescue

The Bridesmaid Rescue

The Girl Next Door Rescue

The Secret Crush Rescue

The Bachelorette Rescue

The Maid By Mistake Rescue

The Unlucky Bride Rescue

———

Black Tie Billionaires

written exclusively by Jo Grafford

Her Billionaire Champion — a Prequel

Her Billionaire Boss

Her Billionaire Bodyguard

Her Billionaire Secret Admirer

Her Billionaire Best Friend

Her Billionaire Geek

Her Billionaire Double Date

———

Heart Lake

written exclusively by Jo Grafford

Winds of Change

Song of Nightingales

Perils of Starlight

Billionaire Birthday Club

(a multi-author series)

Titles by Jo:

The Billionaire's Birthday Date

The Billionaire's Birthday Blind Date

The Billionaire's Birthday Secret

Billionaire Birthday Club Box Set

Mail Order Brides Rescue Series

written exclusively by Jo Grafford

Hot-Tempered Hannah

Cold-Feet Callie

Fiery Felicity

Misunderstood Meg

Dare-Devil Daisy

Outrageous Olivia

Jinglebell Jane

Absentminded Amelia

Bookish Belinda

Tenacious Trudy

Meddlesome Madge

Mismatched MaryAnne

MOB Rescue Series Box Set Books 1-4

MOB Rescue Series Box Set Books 5-8

MOB Rescue Series Box Set Books 9-12

———

Mail Order Brides of Christmas Mountain

written exclusively by Jo Grafford

Bride for the Innkeeper

Bride for the Deputy

Bride for the Tribal Chief

———

Angel Creek Christmas Brides

(a multi-author series)

Titles by Jo:

Elizabeth

Grace

Lilly

———

Once Upon a Church House Series

written exclusively by Jo Grafford

Abigail

Rachel

Naomi

Esther

The Lawkeepers

(a multi-author series)

Titles by Jo:

Lawfully Ours

Lawfully Loyal

Lawfully Witnessed

Lawfully Brave

Lawfully Courageous

Widows, Brides, and Secret Babies

(a multi-author series)

Titles by Jo:

Mail Order Mallory

Mail Order Isabella

Mail Order Melissande

Christmas Rescue Series

(a multi-author series)

Title by Jo:

Rescuing the Blacksmith

———

Border Brides

(a multi-author Series)

Titles by Jo:

Wild Rose Summer

Going All In

Herd the Heavens

———

The Pinkerton Matchmaker

(a multi-author series)

Titles by Jo:

An Agent for Bernadette

An Agent for Lorelai

An Agent for Jolene

An Agent for Madeleine

———

Lost Colony Series

written exclusively by Jo Grafford

Breaking Ties

Trail of Crosses

Into the Mainland

Higher Tides

_____

Ornamental Match Maker Series

(a multi-author series)

Titles by Jo:

Angel Cookie Christmas

Star-Studded Christmas

Stolen Heart Valentine

Miracle for Christmas in July

Home for Christmas

_____

Whispers In Wyoming

(a multi-author series)

Titles by Jo:

His Wish, Her Command

His Heart, Her Love

_____

Silverpines

(a multi-author series)

Titles by Jo:

Wanted: Bounty Hunter

The Bounty Hunter's Sister

———

Brides of Pelican Rapids

(a multi-author series)

Title by Jo:

Rebecca's Dream

———

Sailors and Saints

(a multi-author series)

Title by Jo:

The Sailor and the Surgeon